THE DAUGHTER OF
ARTEMIS

To : Kris Fox

From: Izabella Castillo

THE DAUGHTER OF
ARTEMIS

The Trainer

IZABELLA CASTILLO

Library of Congress Control Number:		2019917307
ISBN:	Hardcover	978-1-7960-6743-9
	Softcover	978-1-7960-6742-2
	eBook	978-1-7960-6741-5

Print information available on the last page.

Rev. date: 10/23/2019

To order additional copies of this book, contact:
Xlibris
1-888-795-4274
www.Xlibris.com
Orders@Xlibris.com
804781

CHAPTER 1

On May 15, 1465, the Princess of England was born. Her mother, Queen Mary, was twenty years old. She had auburn hair and brilliant green eyes. Her father, King Phillip, was twenty-three. He had brown hair and brown eyes.

"She's gorgeous," He mused. "And full of grace" Her mother sighed. They thought of names for minutes, even hours and then, Mary gasped. "Darling, what's wrong?" Phillip asked. "Grace Lilian Evans is her name," she breathed. Princess Grace grew up to be a beautiful girl with long auburn hair like her mother's and dark brown eyes, like her father's. She had freckles across her nose.

Now Grace was twelve years old and she always wanted to explore and ride her horse, Rose. She would eat a healthy and delicious breakfast, then go hunting in her favorite part of the woods. She would ride her horse or wander the halls and talk to her favorite maid, Clara. Princess Grace had a normal life, for now...

CHAPTER 2

One day, Grace was wandering the endless halls of the castle, lit by several golden torches, when she took a wrong turn.

Where am I? She thought.

Suddenly, she heard a voice singing, in fact, the most beautiful voice she'd ever heard, but then her father yelled, "Grace!!" and came striding down the halls so fast that he knocked into all the maids and did not say a word to them. He came up to her and said, "May I speak to you in private?" He asked gripping Grace's arm forcefully. But Grace knew it wasn't a question. She followed her father into a small room but could still hear the faint singing coming from the end of the hall.

"What were you thinking wandering off like that?" he roared, his brown eyes flashing.

"I'm sorry father I took a wrong turn and then heard singing," she whispered.

"Nonsense, go to your room now," he yelled.

"But father," Grace pleaded.

"No. I will not hear it," he yelled pointing to the door.

CHAPTER 3

Grace stomped to her room and slammed the door. She flopped onto her bed with a sigh. Her room was painted royal blue with beautiful gold trim; she had a huge canopy bed with a wood roof and an oak desk.

"This is so unfair," she muttered

A few minutes later, there was a knock on the door.

"Don't come in," Grace snapped. The door opened anyway, it was her mother.

"Are you okay, Grace?" her mother asked, her green eyes full of concern.

"No. I heard singing and father wouldn't even let me explain anything," she complained looking out her window towards the shooting range.

"Well to cheer you up I brought some blueberry tarts and good news," she insisted.

"Today is Friday! And guess what? Tomorrow is your thirteenth birthday party, because your real birthday is on Wednesday and no one is available on a weekday, but it is still an important time in a young woman's life," she announced.

"Oh no! I completely forgot that it was tomorrow! I need to plan an outfit and go to ballroom dance class and-" Her mother cut her off.

"Grace, relax okay it's all been arranged your dress fitting is at eleven, lunch and cake testing is at one, and ballroom at five so you can rest in between," she explained calmly. Her mother left and Grace sighed.

CHAPTER 4

Grace woke to the sound of church bells, which she usually thought sounded beautiful, but today it made her nauseous. Wow I'm thirteen. She thought. She pulled on her hunting outfit, her favorite blue stockings, and a black long sleeve tunic. She marched toward the door and grabbed her willow bow and her hand carved arrows. She almost bumped into her favorite maid, Clara on her way out.

Clara was about sixty years old and the sweetest woman you've ever met, she had greying hair and bright blue eyes that can be stern and affectionate.

"Oh, I'm so sorry, Clara. Can you tell my parents that I'll be back in time for brunch?" Grace asked.

"Of course, sweetie, and Happy birthday!" Clara responded.

"Thank you!" Grace yelled as she ran out.

A few hours later, Grace returned tired from the hunt. She walked into her room and sat at her wood desk, she glanced at the clock above her door. It was 10:55!

"I'm going to be late and it's a dress fitting for the most important party of my life!" she moaned.

She hopped up and ran to her closet and started scanning the closet for her flowing peach dress. Finally, she found it. She slipped it on, pulled her hair out of its loose braid and pushed on a black headband, and on her way out, she put on her black flats.

CHAPTER 6

Meanwhile, in the castle Queen Mary was in the ballroom watching the progress of the servants setting up everything for the party.

"Can you put that banner a smidge to the left?" she asked the servants.

"Clara?" The queen looked around. "Yes, Mary?" Clara asked. "I am going to leave you in charge while I'm getting ready. Then I think you can go get ready. And I am sure Poppy will be more than happy to help. (Poppy was thirty-five year old woman with blond hair and precisely the same shade of brown eyes as Lily. She was Lily's mother.)" She said in quite a rush.

"Of course, ma'am leave it all to me," Clara smiled.

"Thank you, Clara," The queen walked off.

She opened the door to her room and there was a woman, she wasn't solid almost like water.

"Hello Artemis," the woman said calmly.

Mary did not even seem surprised that a woman that looked like a ghost was in her bedroom.

"It's Mary I'll have you know," Mary replied coldly.

"You are not fooling anyone, Artemis. I have come to warn you. She is turning thirteen today, you must tell her," The shimmering woman commanded.

"No, she is safe this way," Mary said firmly.

"This is my final warning, Artemis," And the woman vanished.

Mary sat down on her bed, shaking not from fear but anger. Mary suddenly gasped and crumpled.

In her room, Grace and Emma were putting on their dresses. Emma's dress was a dark blue chiffon dress and had spaghetti straps. She had made it herself, but told Grace that it took no time. (Though as she put it on, she looked extremely pleased.) Grace laced up her dress and turned around. Emma's jaw dropped.

"You look gorgeous!" She exclaimed.

Grace's dress was a long sleeve lace over white silk, it went to the floor in layers and laced up the back.

"Really? You think so?" Grace asked.

"Think?! I know! You look absolutely gorgeous! I can barely stand it!" Emma yelled. "Now for makeup," She insisted, pulling Grace over to the desk. They dumped out the bag of makeup Queen Mary had given them onto the desk. Grace grabbed her mirror and propped it on the desk, the girls sat down and began doing their makeup. Then, the girls put on their nicest jewelry and walked out the door and down the hall.

CHAPTER 7

King Phillip dropped to his knees to his Queen's side, he picked her up and set her gently on the bed.

"CLARA!!!!!" He yelled, so loud in fact everyone in the castle could hear him. Clara came rushing in and when she saw the queen shivering and pale she almost turned as white as the queen. "I'll be right back sir," She muttered, rushing out the door. Clara returned minutes later with the Doctor, a nurse, Lily, and Poppy, along with Grace and Emma. The doctor ran to the Queen's side, nodded at the nurse and pulled out his bag, the maid went out the door and came back with water, tea and a hot cloth. The nurse started checking the Queen's temperature and laying out supplies. Grace looked at her father.

"What happened to her?" She asked urgently.

"We don't know yet," He responded shaking his head.

"Is there anything I can do?" Emma asked.

"No dear, I don't think so," Clara assured sweetly.

In a matter of minutes, the Queen was awake.

"Mother, are you okay? What happened? Should we cancel the birthday? I mean, what's going on?" Grace babbled.

"Oh dear, it's nothing serious, and to answer your questions, yes. I am perfectly fine, nothing to concern yourself with, and no, we shall not cancel." Grace looked at her mother, worried. The King and Queen led Emma, Lily, and Poppy downstairs to the ballroom. Everybody walked down stairs except for Grace and Clara. King Phillip stood up,

"You have all been invited here today to celebrate my daughter Princess Grace Lilian Evans' thirteenth Birthday Ball!" He announced. Everyone cheered. The queen stood up next to king and they both waved and smiled.

"When they say "Princess Grace," you walk down the stairs and Emma will take you to your throne," She explained. She turned and smiled "Good Luck," And then walked away.

"I give you, Princess Grace!" Her father roared, and everyone cheered.

Grace walked down the stairs slowly when she was halfway down, Emma walked to the foot of the stairs. When Grace got to the bottom Emma linked arms with her.

"How do you feel?" She asked quietly.

"Sort of like I'm going to throw up," She whispered under her breath.

"That's perfectly natural," Emma whispered.

They both laughed, and Emma let go at the bottom of the stairs and curtsied. As Grace looked around at the crowd, she felt like she was going to faint. But, she quickly shook herself out of it and plastered on a fake smile.

The Ball was lovely, there was a chocolate fountain with strawberries. There were over thirty windows and the view through them was gorgeous. Out the window you could see the entire kingdom. Grace and Emma walked around until Emma started chatting with a seamstress from another kingdom. Grace muttered something about getting a drink and walked off, smiling. When Grace reached the drinks, a prince from another kingdom walked up to her.

"Princess Grace, a pleasure," The boy bowed, his light grey eyes piercing hers. Grace smiled and curtsied.

"The pleasure is all mine," Grace assured the boy, smiling when actually her mind was wildly trying to remember what her etiquette teacher Hannah had taught her the previous day.

"Prince Noah, at your service," Noah had tousled black hair and pale skin. His breeches black and his gold buttoned coat the color of the ocean.

"Lovely to meet you, Noah," Grace nodded, taking a sip of her drink and staring at Emma talking to a blonde haired boy who seemed to have just asked her to dance.

"Must be exciting, being thirteen," Noah smiled, also grabbing a drink from the table. "And you aren't or weren't?" Grace asked, looking Noah up and down.

Noah laughed. Grace couldn't tell if she should laugh or frown and compromised by choking on her drink.

As he patted Grace's back, he said, "It's a bit complicated, you see," Noah began.

"I'm sure it is," Grace muttered.

The prince cocked a smile. "I just turned fourteen not too long ago. But, on my thirteenth birthday, I forgot. Because my brother had just gone to war, so I was a little distracted," Grace opened her mouth to laugh but then closed it when she realized she had almost forgotten her thirteenth birthday as well.

"When will your brother be crowned King?" Grace asked, changing the subject. Noah looked up at Grace, his stone colored eyes clouding over with sadness.

"Grace, my brother, Ethan was killed during the war," Noah said, looking off.

Grace heard herself gasped slightly. "Noah, I'm so sorry. I had no idea," Grace muttered softly.

Noah turned to her and managed a smile. "No problem. I'll see you around, Princess," Noah said earnestly, though he walked away quickly.

Grace felt horrible. She couldn't imagine what it was like for Noah when he found out his brother was gone. And here I am, talking about it with him. That's probably why he left. Grace thought miserably. Then, she saw a piece of parchment by her left hand. It had the name of Noah's castle on it. Grace grinned. Emma walked up to Grace, also smiling. The girls exchanged stories then, danced and had dessert.

"This cake is divine!!" Grace gushed. "I know!" Emma agreed. Then, Grace thought about the singing she had heard not that long ago. "I need to use the restroom," Grace said quickly. Emma winked and Grace walked off, but she beelined toward the door instead. She looked around and then closed the door quietly behind her.

CHAPTER 8

Grace crept down the hall, which was very hard to do in Glass Slippers!

"Curse you, you beautiful glass slippers!" She muttered. She was halfway down the hall when someone's hand grabbed her shoulder. She jumped.

"It's just me, Grace," Came a voice, Grace recognized was Emma's. "But also, what are you doing out here?" She asked her eyebrows furrowing.

"Fine," Grace muttered. She explained everything the singing, how her father wouldn't listen. Emma listened intently and clung on to every single word Grace said.

"Well then, let's go to the voice," Emma decided.

"Really? Serious?" Grace exclaimed. "Of course," Emma nodded. They walked down the twisting halls and finally they heard it, it was faint but it was loud enough for them to follow it. Once they got close they realized there wasn't a door it was just a bookshelf dimly lit by a torch. Grace began running her fingers along the books, a specific one caught her eye it was old leather and had gold writing but it wasn't in English. It read κίνδυνος. She pulled on it but instead of coming out, the bookshelf turned to the side just enough to let them slip through. They stepped through and the bookshelf went back into place. They walked down and Grace was so scared she didn't realize Emma was squeezing her arm.

"I'm scared, Grace," Emma whispered.

"You're telling me," Grace hissed, glaring at her. Emma let go guiltily. Grace walked forward, rubbing her arm. The singing grew louder. All of the sudden, Emma stopped as if there was a border between her and Grace.

"GRACE!!!" Emma yelled. But Grace couldn't hear her, and she kept walking. Then Grace came upon a door, she opened it without hesitation. Inside, there was a crystal bowl. Next to the bowl was a woman but she wasn't a woman just a ghostly shimmer of one, she had long black hair and a dress the colors of a peacock.

"ποιος είσαι?" Grace demanded, coming out of a trance. All of the sudden Grace realized she hadn't been speaking in English, and she fainted immediately. The woman sighed and waved her hand. Instantly, Grace was awake and horrified.

"But you, I... how-" Grace stuttered, pointing at the woman.

"To answer your question, χάρη, I am Hera, goddess of the heavens," She explained calmly. Grace somehow knew that when the woman had said a word in whatever language she was speaking she had said Grace.

"That's impossible," Grace nodded in disbelief.

"Oh, but it is, your mother is Artemis, goddess of the hunt and the moon," Hera argued, getting directly to the point. "And you will be cursed at midnight," Hera said in a bored kind of way as if she did this all the time. All of this settled into Grace's mind.

"And I am just supposed to believe you? But if it is true..." Grace trailed off. "How do I get rid of the curse? What, in fact is the curse?" Grace babbled peppering Hera with questions. Hera smiled coldly. This sent a shiver down Grace's back.

"Oh Grace, so young, so innocent. You cannot get rid of the curse. Oh and, the curse is that at midnight next Wednesday you will gain all of your mother's power and it will be too much for you to handle even for a child of the gods. You will have to find a way to control all of the power in ten days at most, before it overwhelms you and you burn up," Hera said smiling, still ever so coldly.

Grace began to cry, tears silently sliding down her face.

"Well, I do suppose you could go to Chiron, trainer of Achilles, son of Kronos, wisest and eldest of the Kentauros," Hera insinuated casually.

"Where is he?" Grace asked fiercely.

"Now, now that isn't anyway to speak to a Goddess is it?" Hera smiled, her voice sweet and light, though her blue eyes flashed dangerously.

"I don't care!" Grace exclaimed. "I'm about to get burnt out and you're getting all fired up about how I speak to you?!?!?!" Grace yelled.

Hera's smile faded quickly. She looked directly into Grace's eyes, blue to brown. Grace saw her 10th birthday when her parents had such a huge row they had not spoken to each other for a week, when her grandmother had died only a year ago and she placed a beautiful silver and diamond charm bracelet in Grace's hand, and Grace's first horse, Summer, dying.

Then, Grace was on the ground sobbing, holding the bracelet her grandmother had given her.

"Do not test me, little girl," Hera said curtly. "Now, I see that coming here was a waste of time, you do not understand the power of the gods and you do not appreciate it. Maybe letting you have the burden of a goddess yourself will teach you a lesson," Hera snapped, her eyes cold as ice yet blazing as a bonfire. She dissolved on the spot.

CHAPTER 9

Grace ran past the crystal bowl, through the door, back to the place where Emma had let go. Grace had completely forgotten about Emma until now. She wondered if Emma was okay, if Hera had taken her to make Grace lose even more hope. Grace's heart skipped a beat. But when she got back to that spot, Emma was still there sobbing very loudly; her brown hair had come down from its elegant knot and was sticking to her tear stained face, and her eyeliner and mascara were also running down her face and onto her dress. Grace thought she must not look any better than Emma after everything she'd been through in the past forty- five minutes.

"Emma, I am so sorry. I shouldn't have dragged you into this. It's my fault, I am the worst best friend ever," Grace apologized, basically in tears again.

Emma looked Grace full in the face, and there was an odd expression on her face. It was a mixture of confusion, curiosity, and understanding. She gave Grace a crooked smile.

"No need to apologize, Grace. Just tell me where we're going, what were doing, and I will be there with you every step of the way," Emma promised.

Grace took in a deep breath and let everything out. Half an hour later, Emma stood up and pulled Grace into a big hug. They walked down the hall, to the right, the left, and the left one last time and they were back to the party. Grace walked in and walked straight up to her mother.

"Mother, may I have a word?" Grace asked politely. Mary turned around and smiled. She jumped.

"Of course, my dear. But first, what happened to you?" Mary asked, looking slightly alarmed.

"Nothing, I know that you're Artemis. I know about the curse and I need your help to find Chiron," Grace said rather impatiently.

Mary looked her in the eyes.

"Well, I guess you were going to find out soon enough," Mary sighed. "Go into my room, find the jewelry box pick up the jewelry tray and under that there will be a letter, that will explain everything. You must go!" Mary explained.

"Mom, we can't go," Grace pleaded. "GO" Mary responded firmly. "Emma?" Grace asked. "Ready," Emma replied, taking Grace by the hand and pulling her out the door. They walked down the hall. Soon enough they were in the Queen's bedroom. It was all red and white, with a large bed. They walked past the bed towards the dresser. The jewelry box was polished walnut with the moon phases carved into it. Emma opened the lid; it was filled with beautiful gold and silver. Grace moved forward and picked up the jewelry tray, under it there was a dozen pieces of paper, but on top was an envelope that looked at least twelve years old. Grace picked it up and opened it, it said, in her mother's neat handwriting:

Dear Grace, I am so sorry. I should have told you earlier. I am Artemis, goddess of the hunt and the moon. You will be cursed. You will get all my powers and it will burn you out. You must find the trainer, Chiron. You can take a friend with you if they wear this chain necklace at all times. Magic borders will separate you and anyone else that is not magical. Now, here is a map to Chiron. Find him. He will train you to control the powers. Wear this necklace with a crescent charm, use my bow, and put this barrette in your hair. I love you so much, never forget it. GO!

CHAPTER 10

There was a small box in the jewelry box. The box was small and it contained 2 necklaces, a barrette, and a compass.

"We have to use this compass to find the bow and arrows," Emma guessed.

"Yeah, I think you're right," Grace agreed.

Emma grabbed the compass and pointed north. They followed the compass through the endless halls. Finally, they reached the bow and it was beautiful. It was made of grey wood. It also had the moon phases carved into the side.

Grace frowned, "There are no arrows," But she grabbed the bow anyway and pulled her red hair into a long plait.

Emma put her brown hair into a ponytail. Grace put the barrette into her hair; it was the shape of an arrow. The necklace her mother had left her was a silver moon on a silver chain. The necklace she left for Emma was a plain silver chain. Once they were ready, the girls basically ran to Grace's room.

Grace got out 3 rucksacks, "Do you have any clothes? Here are some of mine," Grace offered. She started handing Emma clothes. Emma took them gratefully. When they were both packed, they both got up and crept out the door.

"What is the third bag for?" Emma whispered.

"Food," Grace whispered back.

They crept to the kitchen, and started grabbing all the food they could.

"Don't forget to take some meat pies," It was Clara. Her blue eyes had a strange twinkle to them. Clara took the bag from them and started filling it with food.

"Oh Clara, how could I ever repay you?" Grace asked.

"You can stay safe. Now go," Clara responded. She shoved the bag into Grace's arms and hugged her tightly, then hugged Emma, too.

"Let's go," Emma commanded swinging a sack over her back and looking at Grace. They walked to the front, took a deep breath, opened the great oak doors and walked into the darkness.

CHAPTER 11

Grace grabbed a torch from the side of the door. The torch amber light lit up the cold and vast night. As they walked, Grace wondered if she would ever walk into these doors ever again. They finally reached the horse stables. Emma put the sacks into the saddlebags.

"Here you can ride Pumpkin," Grace offered Emma. Grace helped Emma onto Pumpkin, a brown horse with a blond mane.

Then Grace herself, climbed onto Rose, her horse, Rose was light brown with a pure white mane and Grace often braided roses into her mane and tail. Grace opened the map. It had all kinds of terrain, mountains, plains, lakes, and forests. There was an X in a part called the Forest of the Kentauros. Grace and Emma assumed that Chiron was there.

"But, it looks like the forest and everything around it is pretty rough," Emma pointed out.

Grace looked at the map, Emma was right. She felt a sinking feeling in the pit of her stomach. There were troll mountains, snake plains, siren lakes, and other awful things.

"Well then, we better get going if we're going to have this much bad ahead of us," Grace cringed, trying to keep her and Emma's spirits up.

They trotted along the forest for a while.

"Grace, where are we? We should stop soon, the sun is going down and we shouldn't be out here in the dark, I mean I've read quite a lot about Greek mythology and we do not want to encounter any of those monsters," Emma reassured.

"You're right," Grace sighed.

Emma glanced at the map, there was a small town just east of them. "Alright then, looks like we are going to be spending a night or two in a town called Tunbridge," They rode for a few minutes at the least. Then, there was a clearing in the forest. There was a small town it had stores, houses, and blacksmiths. Grace saw a woman, she looked around 20, she was very pretty with caramel hair and blue eyes. She was wearing a long white dress and brown shoes. Grace and Emma walked over to the woman.

"Hello, I'm Grace, and this is my friend Emma. We need a place to stay. Do you know of any places we could stay for the night?" Grace asked politely. The woman stared at them for a minute, as if not sure what she was seeing.

"Well, I suppose I do. My name is Amelia. You can stay with me and my husband!" Amelia offered.

"Thanks so much!" Grace said, a little confused. They got their horses and walked to Amelia's house. It was a small cottage with stucco and a straw roof. They walked into the house. There was a man.

"These lovely girls will be staying at our house for the night," Amelia announced.

"Brilliant to meet you, our names are Grace and Emma," Grace said, smiling.

"Hello girls, it's a pleasure to meet you. I am James, Amelia's husband," Smiled James, he looked 25 with blonde hair, brown eyes. He also looked at them a little strangely.

"Well girls I'll show you your room and then get started on supper," Amelia said, tucking her caramel hair behind her ears. She walked up to the third door in the cottage. She pushed it open and it creaked slightly. Inside there were 2 trundle beds, a dresser and a small window.

"Thank you, Amelia," Emma thanked her sincerely.

Amelia smiled and closed the door behind her. They laid out their clothes in silence. Then the girls laid down for a nap. Once out of bed, Grace smacked her head.

"What!?!?!" Emma asked, looking alarmed.

"We didn't even clean up before we left!" Grace said, half laughing. "That's why Amelia and James were looking at us like we were mad!"

The girls laughed for a while. After this, the girls washed their faces and changed their clothes. Then, they walked out for supper.

"Thank you so much, Amelia. I hope you didn't go to too much trouble to cook extra for us," Grace blushed.

"No, no trouble at all dear," Amelia reassured Grace.

They ate their potatoes, bread, and cheese quickly. Then they trudged off to bed.

The next morning, they awoke early. Grace's hair was down and curly from her braid. She wore a pale blue knee length dress with black tights, tall brown lace up boots and a black and gold cloak. Emma's hair was down and straight. She wore a white blouse, red skirt, black boots, and a red cloak. They had toast and jam for breakfast.

"Amelia, we can't thank you enough," Emma said.

Grace stepped forward and handed Amelia a great big bag of gold. Amelia's blue eyes widened.

"Thank you so much!" Amelia gushed.

The girls said their farewells. The girls walked around the house to the stables and grabbed their horses, Pumpkin and Rose.

They rode through the town for a while. Finally, they reached the town limit.

"Emma, could you take a look at the map and see where we could stay?" Grace asked lightly.

"Of course, give me one moment," Emma muttered, rummaging through her bag. She pulled it out and began examining it. "Well, it looks like there is a castle, not far from here. They might let us stay there, seeing as they probably have more room than Amelia and James had," Emma smiled.

"Probably," Grace laughed. "Do you have an estimate of how far it is?" She continued seriously.

"Looks like it might be around a ten minute ride from here," Emma declared happily, smiling down at the map.

"Then, we better get going," Grace said.

They rode for what seemed like the time Emma had said they would have arrived. Finally, they reached the Bodiam Castle. Emma gasped.

CHAPTER 12

Grace and Emma both had expected it to be beautiful and full of life, instead it was the exact opposite. It was crumbling, there were dark curtains in every window, and on the highest tower there were thick metal bars instead of glass.

"It's hideous!" Emma blurted.

Grace looked over at her and Emma blushed.

"You are correct. But it is the most sacred castle and has a ton of incredibly history. It is owned by the Jones, one of the most powerful royal families in all of Britain," Grace muttered staring around breathlessly.

They rode up, and once they were at the door, Grace and Emma knocked at the same time. The door opened, and standing inside was a man. He looked around Clara's age, he had brown eyes and grey hair. He had a slightly crazed look in his eyes.

"Welcome to the Jones' humble abode," He said, his mouth barely moving and bowing. But there was a lot of fear in his voice.

Grace and Emma looked at each other, raising their eyebrows. Grace shrugged.

"Allow me, to take you lovely maidens to the Queen Evelyn," He said bowing again, and leading the girls out of the room.

The castle was odd. There was a cold chill and a strange mist, all of the castles most precious artifacts were covered in dirt. Grace, Emma, and the man passed several maids that also had a frightened air about them. Finally, they reached the dining hall. The strange man led them into the hall. It was just as cold and ugly as the rest of the castle. In the dining hall, there was a huge stone table it could probably sit 60 people. But in front of it there was a small marble table that could maybe fit 8 people at the most. At the table was a family, the Jones. King George had blond hair and grey eyes, he was looking at the dusty chandelier, not meeting the girl's eyes. Queen Evelyn had curled black hair and intense green eyes, almost like a snake. Princess Daisy had long blond hair and brown eyes, she seemed to be on the verge of tears. Grace and Emma looked at each other. Prince Daniel, Princess Daisy's twin also had blond hair and brown eyes, he was also looking very grim. Queen Evelyn glided toward them.

"Welcome girls. Are you looking to stay the night?" Queen Evelyn asked smoothly.

"Yes actually, if it isn't too much trouble for you," Emma replied politely, curtsying.

"No, no trouble at all, I- um we, would be absolutely thrilled to have you stay with us. Now, sit down, relax, enjoy," She said in a falsely bright voice.

Emma and Grace both curtsied then sat down at the table, smiling. The Queen was the only one besides Emma and Grace that didn't have a frightened look in their eyes. The girls began eating greedily and fast. When they were finished Emma and Grace stood up. Queen Evelyn smiled, her forked tongue flicked out. Emma and Grace screamed, horrified. Evelyn cackled.

"Echidna?!?!?!" Grace gasped.

"Yes. It is I, Echidna, killer of men, devourer of all animals and humans," Echidna said, loudly.

"But what about the real Queen Evelyn?" Grace asked.

Echidna gave a cold laugh.

"Her? I finished her off a long time ago," Echidna sneered.

"Well, I would devour you both now but I have a full castle of people to eat. You two are dessert, so I must feed you and then I will devour your bodies and your souls. Guards!!!!! Take them to the dungeon!!!!!" Echidna hissed, literally.

Three men burst into the room grabbing Grace and Emma by the arms. Echidna's cackling grew fainter as they walked along the creepy halls, the guards led them to a wood door with metal latches.

The first guard turned to the other two. "The she-demon said these two are supposed to be locked in cell number sixty-three, you know the one with that girl,"

"Yes sir, right away sir," The third guard stammered, nodding at the second guard. The first guard walked away. Guard three and two walked Grace and Emma to cell sixty-three.

In the cell, was a girl. She looked the same age as Grace and Emma with shoulder length choppy brown hair and her eyes were a mix of blue, green, and yellow. The guards threw them roughly into the cell.

The girl jumped when Grace spoke to her. "Hello, my name is Grace and this is my friend, Emma,"

"Oh, Hello, my name is Olivia," The girl said quietly, not looking at the girls.

"How did you end up in here? We had no idea that it was Echidna," Emma said politely.

"Well, my parents, my brother, and I were all thrown in here, because my dad wouldn't give her our cows. She took them anyway and when my dad kept trying to escape, that was the last straw for her. She took my dad, my mother, and my brother. She killed and ate all of them, she said I wasn't old enough," Olivia lamented.

"Oh Olivia, I am so sorry. But don't worry we are going to break out of here soon. Well, at least until I find out all the hinges and locks. Do not worry," Grace reassured her. Olivia smiled.

"Good luck and good night," Olivia sighed.

Grace realized that the girl, Olivia, wasn't trying to be mean, she had just tried this for years without any luck. Grace and Emma agreed to get some rest and find a way to escape tomorrow. The girls drifted off to sleep in the tiny cell. The next morning Grace, Emma, and Olivia were awakened by the sound of a scream. A horrible, high, piercing scream, it came from a woman. Grace and Emma thought maybe Echidna had started eating the castle workers. But as they listened they realized it was coming from Echidna herself, she was angry, very, very angry. All of the sudden footsteps were coming towards cell sixty-three.

"Yes General, someone stole the keys. But it could not have been just anyone, General.

Only very few people know where it is hidden, sir," Came a nervous voice, around the corner, so the inmates in cell sixty-three couldn't see who it was.

"Well, then go check the cell, dimwit," Came the General's rough voice.

"Yes, sir, right on it, sir," Stammered the other voice. Light footsteps came towards the cell.

"Do you guys have weapons? We may need to kill," Olivia muttered under her breath, stepping in front of Grace and Emma.

"Well, no. I mean I have a bow, just not any arrows," Grace whispered, turning red. Olivia turned around and looked at them quizzically.

"Back corner of the cell, under the hay. I have a few knifes. Grab those and be ready," Olivia commanded. Grace grabbed a knife and Emma found a knife that was perfect for her. Olivia pushed Grace and Emma to the other side of the cell, so when the guard looked in, it seemed as though no one was in there and then they would ambush. But, instead of a guard it was a short, cloaked figure.

"I am here to rescue you guys. Please don't kill me, I am here to help you guys, please," Grace, Emma, and Olivia realized it was the nervous voice from around the corner. Olivia jumped out grabbed the cloaked figure by the robe and put the knife to his neck, her brown eyes full of hate.

"Who are you? What might you have to offer us? Oh, and how exactly do you plan to break us out of here, huh?" Olivia spat.

"Ok, ok, listen," The cloaked figure was definitely a male. "First, I am your savior, you're welcome. Second, I have the keys to break you out of here," The figure explained.

"Alright, break us out of here," Olivia demanded.

The figure set off to work, fumbling through keys, trying them, and sighing.

"May I try that? You don't seem to have memorized the keys," Emma asked, her tone light but her golden eyes irritated.

"So much for a rescue," Grace muttered to Olivia. Olivia gave a small smile, but then turned to the figure.

"Sure, I'd like to see you try," The figure scoffed. Emma glared at them for a second and then snatched the keys out of their hands. She set off to work. Emma looked through the keys then, she picked one out. She handed it to the figure. He stuck it in the lock, and turned it. There was a small click. They were free!

CHAPTER 13

"How did you find it?" the figure asked, astonished.

"Easy. Now I think we ought to get going," Emma said, pulling her hair into a bun. Grace put hers back in its long plait and clipped in the barrette.

"Down here, General! The traitor and the inmates are down here! They've escaped!" Called a guard, thundering down the stairs.

"Excuse me. If we are going to trust you with our lives, and we don't know if you are actually here to help us, can we at least know what your name is? Or what you look like?" Grace urged.

"Now? Really? You know I- you know what, never mind. Okay. Just give me a sec," He responded irritably. "Hello, my name is Leo. A pleasure to meet you all," He said his voice full of sarcasm. "And you will see what I look like in one minute. Ok, we are going to take out these guards, then grab your stuff and head out. Hopefully, without dying," Leo declared.

"Great. Splendid. Brilliant. Amazing. Now, do you have any swords we can borrow? I don't think we can take out, what, ten guards with handcuffs and little knives. No offense, Olivia," Emma added.

"None taken, but you would be surprised at what five little knifes could do to a person," Olivia gave a hollow smile putting a delicate amount of strain on the word. She grabbed all her knifes from under the hay and the ones from Emma and Grace. Five actually. Then, Olivia stood against the wall, waiting. Leo threw a sword at the ground at each Grace and Emma's feet. They picked them up with a little difficulty then, hid. Ten guards came down the steps. Olivia threw three of her knifes with deadly accuracy, one hit a guard right in the heart, one of the other two landed in one guards stomach, the other one knocked their weapon right out of his hand. Two guards down, eight to go. Leo jumped out of his hiding spot and threw his cloak off, he had dark brown hair and blue eyes. His tan arms had a few thin red marks across them, as if someone had whipped him. He charged. He put a deep gash in one guard's cheek, then, kicked his weapon out of his hand. And cut one of the guard's hands off, Grace and Emma cringed. Two more guards down six to go. Grace, Emma, Olivia, and Leo all charged at the same time. Swords clashed, knifes flew, and guards fell to the ground. Emma was amazing, she slashed, parried, and spun. Grace had never seen Emma fight so fiercely. Emma took out three guards, while handcuffed! That left one guard for Grace, Olivia, and Leo. Everyone fought with such in intensity. When all ten guards were finished, Leo grabbed the keys and took off the girl's handcuffs. Then, they grabbed their stuff and ran out. Echidna was screaming at the guards.

"You know what? I am not going to help you kill innocent people!" one of the guards yelled fiercely.

"Oh, is that the way you feel, hmmm?" Echidna sneered. "Well, then I think you ought to die!" she screamed.

The guards charged at her, she scratched, bit, and killed. A moment later, all the guards were laying on the floor, dead.

"How are we going to defeat her? She killed ten guards in a minute," Leo said pointedly.

"We'll just try our best, I mean we killed ten guards in three minutes," Grace insisted.

They stepped out into Echidna's view.

"So, the little heroes escaped. Well, I'm not sure they'll make it passed here," Echidna threatened.

Emma, Olivia, and Leo charged but Echidna was equal to all three of them. Grace felt something on the side of her head getting heavier and heavier, until she was in danger of falling one way. She looked at her shoulder and she couldn't believe her eyes! The arrow barrette her mother gave her, grew into an actual arrow! Grace quickly unclipped it and notched it to her bow. She notched the arrow into the bow and pictured herself hunting back home, the tall green trees, the smell of pine, and the chirping of birds. She took her aim, directly at Echidna. She let it fly, and it found its mark. It hit Echidna right in the arm, she hissed and shrieked in pain. Grace shot her arrow again, it just kept reappearing notched in Grace's bow. Grace looked up, Echidna was winning, but she was also fading. Emma ducked under Echidna's taloned hand and swung her sword at Echidna's snake trunk, Leo swung at her body, and Olivia at her head, but Echidna was too quick. She hit Emma with her tail and sent her flying into the wall. She blocked Leo's attack and struck him hard across the face, making him fall to the hard floor. Olivia and Echidna both struck at the same time. Olivia yelped in pain and fell to the floor. Echidna crumbled to dust. Olivia had struck Echidna in the neck, Echidna had pulled a knife out of her sleeve and stuck Olivia in the gut. Grace, Emma, and Leo ran to Olivia's side, she was bleeding pretty bad. Emma looked around frantically. She realized her blouse was made of gauze, she put on her cloak, so no one could see her and changed her shirt. Then, she ripped most of it off and wrapped it around Olivia's stomach. Olivia struggled to her feet.

"Thank you," Olivia said gratefully. Leo put her left arm around his shoulder and Emma put her right on her shoulder. Grace marched forward towards the dining hall doors. Grace and Emma had never seen the General before. His eyes were a silvery grey, and had short brown hair. Grace thought he must have been at least forty years old.

"Well, then hunt them down. Get all of our guards on duty. We must find them," The General commanded urgently.

Grace notched her bow, the way she did with Echidna. She held her breath and let her arrow fly, it hit the guard that was talking to the General in the stomach. He groaned and dropped to his knees at the General's feet, but the General wasn't paying attention to the guard. He was drawing his sword out of its leather scabbard and walking towards Grace. Emma and Leo set Olivia down by the wall.

"Wait," She called feebly. But Emma and Leo had already gone to Grace's aid.

The General swung his sword directly at Grace's neck but Emma caught his sword with her equally quick blade.

"What?" The General exclaimed.

"What?" Emma shot back swinging hard.

"Who are you? How did you escape?" He hissed.

Emma laughed coldly. "We escaped thanks to your "guard" uh...Leo,"

The General whipped around and when he saw Leo and Olivia (Olivia had stood up and was holding all five of her knives.) standing there, fully armed, his expression was priceless.

"You!" He said pointing at Olivia, his face full of hatred.

"Me," She smiled grimly, wincing slightly from the pain in her side.

"And Leo, how could you? You were like a son to me," The General pleaded, but Leo just raised his eyebrows.

"A son you insulted more than ten times a week?" Leo asked coldly. The General was speechless. "What I thought," Leo rebuked.

Grace, Olivia, and Leo each ran to a guard and began fighting like their lives depended on it, which it did. In a matter of minutes, more than half of the guards were dead, wounded, or had run away in fear.

"Surrender! You can never beat us! You are losing men by the minute!" Grace called to the General, shooting down yet another of the General's men. He snarled like a wolf.

"We will see, foolish girl," He glowered. He slashed wildly at Emma, she turned but not in time. His sharp blade caught the side of her shoulder, she looked at her cut; it was bleeding freely. Olivia killed a guard, Leo killed a guard, Grace killed two. They all advanced on the General, shooting, throwing, slashing at him. Then, a woman walked out of a door. She was very beautiful and had shoulder length black hair in perfect ringlets and startling amber eyes. Her skin was pale. Her eyes narrowed slightly at the scene.

"What is going? Where is that horrible monster Echidna? Not that I'm complaining, she was awful. Who are these children? Why are they armed? What are you doing? Oh my god! Why are the guards dead? William?" Her questions were like gunfire, the General stopped in his tracks. So did Grace, Emma, Olivia, and Leo.

"I, uh... Ella...dear," The General stammered. Even considering the amount of danger they were in, Grace had to bite her tongue to refrain from laughing. Dear? Grace thought. The General had a wife? She looked at Olivia on her left and Emma on her right. Emma was, like Grace trying very hard not to laugh out loud. Olivia, on the other hand had a quizzical look on her face.

"Lady Ella, your husband captured us and... oh, we had to defeat Echidna all by ourselves. We are just a bunch of children. I mean look at us," They all lowered their weapons and tried to look innocent.

"Please and now, your husband is going to kill us all," Emma said, willing herself to make fake tears stream down her face. Grace appreciated how good Emma was at being very dramatic.

"What?" Ella asked sharply.

"Yes, it's true, Lady Ella. Please tell your husband to let us go. Please, help us. Tell your husband to let us go, Please," Emma whimpered.

Ella pursed her lips, looking at her husband, then at Grace, Emma, Olivia, and Leo all of whom were staring at her, hopefully.

"Well," she started slowly "I suppose. Very well, William please let them go," Ella soothed.

"Dear, I am afraid I cannot do that. They are criminals. Step aside, Ella," The General- William answered shortly.

"Um... excuse me. You alone do not have the power to decide who or how we punish. I do. They will not end up like our son. I repeat let them go," Ella snapped.

Olivia thinking fast, threw two of her knives at Ella. Ella screamed. The General yelled. Time seemed to slow down as her knives soared directly at Ella.

CHAPTER 14

Everyone held their breath as Olivia's knives flew. Thankfully, her knives did not hit Ella, they merely pinned her to the cobblestone wall. Also thinking fast, The General-William kicked Grace's bow out of her hand and grabbed her, pulling her into his flank. He put the point of his sword to her spine, poised to slice her in half. Leo whipped around. So did Emma. Grace tried to gather herself. Ella and William had a son. Where was he? What had happened to him?

"Let her go, now," Olivia said forcefully. "Or I will show you just how accurately I can throw at your wife," Olivia continued.

"I will let your friend go. If you drop your weapon and release my wife," The General- William maintained.

"Fine. We'll all drop our weapons on three. You will release Grace, then, I will unpin your wife from the wall. Deal?" Olivia asked.

"Deal," The General-William said firmly. "On three then," Leo jumped in. "One, Two, Three," Emma counted.

Everyone dropped their weapons with a clatter. That is everyone, except The General-William. Emma, Olivia, and Leo just noticed this.

"General, put down that weapon and release Grace. You are outnumbered three to one," Olivia cautioned.

"Please if I was truly worried about all of you I would have dropped my weapon," The General-William insinuated. "Release my wife," He continued.

"Give us Grace," Emma said calmly, though she was looking at Olivia then Leo as if waiting for them to say something reassuring. The

General-William opened his mouth to say something, then, closed it. His sword was now pressing very hard on Grace's windpipe, she could hardly breathe. There were stars in front of her eyes. No, you cannot pass out. She thought angrily to herself. Come on, Grace. You are the daughter of a Goddess. You got this. Then, out of nowhere, there was a blinding flash of silver. It was so powerful that Grace, Emma, Olivia, Leo, and The General-William were knocked off their feet. Ella's head hit the hard wall and was knocked out cold. Grace was the first to get up. She looked around, Emma, Olivia, and Leo had started slowly stirring. Unfortunately, so was The General-William. Thick, leathery twine was coming out of both of her hands and wrapping themselves around The General-William. Grace looked down at her hands in pure and utter shock. She fainted out of shock. When Grace woke, Emma, Olivia, and Leo were all staring down at her, looking worried.

"Grace," Began Emma shakily. "W-what was that? And why is The General... tied up? How?" Emma helped Grace to her feet.

"Emma, I do not know how or why The General is tied up," Grace responded wearily. "I mean, there was a blast of silver and then ropes were wrapping themselves around you know... him," Grace babbled, pointing at The General meekly. "And oh, Emma, I think they were coming from me," Grace said quickly.

"Okay, all right, calm down. Just take a deep breath. We'll figure this out," Emma soothed.

"Wait, what? We won't figure this out. Firstly, I would like to know what do you mean, coming from me, Grace?" Olivia demanded. Grace and Emma exchanged weary looks.

"Well, Olivia, Grace's mother is Artemis. And she is cursed that on her thirteenth birthday she will receive all her mother's power... and it will kill her. Literally burn her out. That is, unless she goes to Chiron, the trainer," Emma explained, grimacing, waiting for Olivia to say that she's crazy.

"Then, we need to find this trainer. It sounds serious, but I am up for it," Olivia agreed, looking around for her knives casually, as if she heard that everyday.

"Wait, you believe us?" Grace said, eyes widening. Olivia laughed and picked up her last knife.

"Please, that's the least crazy thing I've heard in my life," Olivia smiled, her eyes twinkling.

"Um... Hello," Leo called, getting the girls attention. Grace, Emma, and Olivia all turned and glared at him. "I never said I would I come with you and besides, you would be lost if it weren't for me," Leo said pointedly. Emma doubled over in silent giggles, Olivia failed at stifling a laugh, and Grace scoffed loudly.

"We never asked you to come. And, if you don't want to then, I suppose we can leave you here to explain what happened to the whole castle. Oh, and you would have to explain to The General," Grace snapped. "If he really likes you, you'll be hung," Grace added as an after-thought, putting her arrow clip back in her hair. To Grace's pleasure, Leo scowled.

"Fine," He assented, though he had a look that plainly said he would rather marry Echidna.

"Excellent. Now that we have got that settled. Let's go," Olivia said hastily, before Grace could respond. Grace stopped glaring at Leo and Leo stopped glaring at Grace. They both turned to look at Emma, who was on the floor holding the cut that The General-William gave her. Everyone had forgotten about the deep cut on Emma's left arm.

"Oh, Emma! I am so sorry," Grace said quickly, not meeting Emma's eyes.

"We forgot," Leo muttered, just as embarrassed as Grace.

"Lucky you," Emma snapped coolly.

"Do you have any more of that fabric you used for me?" Olivia asked Emma, breaking the nasty silence. Grace was relieved, her eyes shot Olivia a quick thank you. Olivia nodded at Grace sympathetically.

"Yes. It's in that sack over there," Said Emma, staring at Grace and Leo slightly angrily. Guilt boiled in Grace's stomach. She looked at Emma and the guilt must have shown in her face because, at this Emma's look softened. Olivia came back with the fabric a second later.

"Thanks, Olivia," Emma smiled.

"No problem. Without this fabric I wouldn't be here to gush over it," Olivia replied. Emma laughed as Olivia wrapped the fabric gently around her arm. Grace noticed that Olivia's expression had changed. It was no longer energetic and fierce, it was concerned, almost motherly. Grace smiled slightly at this.

"What?" Leo demanded.

"Nothing. I'm just pleased we all met, even you Leo," Grace smiled reassuringly. Leo glared at her, but the corners of his mouth twitched.

"Me too," Emma said lightly, finally smiling at Leo and Grace.

"Well, we should get going," Declared Grace.

"Yes. We don't want to wait for the General to wake up, there are still many guards," Olivia agreed.

"Yes, yes. We ought to get going," Emma said, coming out of reverie.

"Yep. Brilliant. Let's go," Leo babbled. They all got up, absorbed in their own thoughts. Grace was feeling many feelings at once. She was still in shock from her powers, guilty about Emma, scared about what would come next, but also pleased about meeting these great friends. And even though Leo got on her nerves, he was rather brilliant. But, of course, she didn't tell him that. They slowly walked out the doors, both Olivia and Emma depending on Grace. Leo dragged behind them carrying the bags. The combined weight of Emma and Olivia was depleting Grace's energy, her eyelids felt heavy. Then, she realized it was not the weight that was tiring her, it was the magic. She guessed a big powerful amount of magic as she did could really take it out of you.

"Take a left right here. And straight, then go through that door. Right, and this door," Olivia directed.

"How do you know how to get out of here so well?" Leo asked, his eyebrows raised. Olivia waved her hand dismissively.

"Oh, you know. I mean... I have lived here for 8 years. I know how to find the chamber room alone," Olivia said airily. Leo blushed. They finally reached the doors where the cowardly man had led them to Echidna. They were made of steel.

"Here," Grace said pointedly, putting both Emma's and Olivia's weight onto his shoulders. Grace almost laughed at Leo's expression. Now he was holding the bags, the weapons, Emma, and Olivia. Grace pulled the door with all her might, she knew soon enough she would fall onto the cold cement floor. Leo laughed.

"You know, you're supposed to push that door, not pull," Now it was time for Grace to blush.

"And you know, you're supposed to be able to recognize keys if you're a guard," Grace snapped, recalling the moment when Leo had forgotten which key opened cell sixty-three. Leo glowered at her but did not seem to have a comeback. Grace allowed herself a satisfied smiled before pushing the metal doors wide. Olivia and Emma leaned on Grace once more as they set off into the cold and dreary afternoon.

"The horse stable is back there," Leo declared, his smug air returned a little faster than Grace would have liked. Leo stepped in front of Grace, Emma, and Olivia and pushed through the brittle dead rose bushes. The garden was just as sad as the castle. Everything was dead and grey.

"You know, I wish we could do something to help the people of this castle," Emma sighed, looking around sadly.

"But, there really isn't Emma. At least Echidna is gone, they'll be really pleased about that. And I think that the King and Ella should be able to exercise some control over The General. Don't you think, Leo?" Olivia asked. Leo looked surprised at being asked his opinion. Grace, Emma, and Olivia smiled at this.

"Yes, yes. Naturally," Leo smiled. They finally reached the horse stables. There was Rose, Pumpkin, a chestnut horse with light brown hair, and a grey horse with a black mane.

"That's Jack and" Leo stopped short, looking over at Olivia.

"Penelope," Olivia finished.

"Brilliant. Well, let's get going," Leo said, opening the gate to his horse.

"Great, you both have horses," Olivia said relieved, also opening her horse's gate. Grace, Emma, Olivia, and Leo all mounted their own horses. They all rode out of stable carefully, into the blood orange sunset.

CHAPTER 15

Once the Moon had come up, Grace felt a surge of strength, the mad urge to get up and go back to fight The General and his entire army. Grace assumed this madness and energy came because her mother was the Goddess of the Moon. Long after twilight, Grace, Emma, Olivia, and Leo rode along a winding road.

Emma yawned. "Do you think we should stop soon? Honestly, I am exhausted,"

"Oh yeah. We should definitely stop. And get killed, as if," Leo scoffed. He received several nasty looks from Grace, Emma, and Olivia.

"As thick headed and arrogant as he is, Leo is right," Olivia sighed.

"Yep. Wait, what?" Leo glowered. Grace laughed but stopped short at the expression on Leo's face. He was looking really downcast, Grace almost felt bad for him.

"Alright. But I'm going to bed anyway. Are you guys going to be good?" Emma asked. Grace nodded.

"Ok. Night all," Emma yawned. She leaned forward, resting her head on Pumpkins neck. They rode for a little longer.

"I really don't want to go to bed, but I can barely keep my eyes open," Olivia cracked.

"Oh, Olivia. You ought to rest. We have a big day ahead of us. Leo and I won't let your horses run off," Grace assured her. Leo looked surprised and pleased that Grace had suggested that he could do something right. Olivia muttered something under her breath but eventually laid her head on top of her horse's mane, like Emma had.

Leo was staring at her. Grace couldn't decide whether she should smile or say something like "You're welcome," She compromised by looking over at Leo and saying

"I know, surprising right? The girl that you've been arguing with the whole day is being nice to you. And standing up for you, and pretty much complimenting you," Leo looked over at Grace and did the last thing that Grace thought he would do. He laughed. He laughed for a few more good long seconds, Grace even got bored listlessly listening to him laugh. Eventually, Grace pulled a small but sharp hunting knife out of her leather boot. She pulled it out of the little holster and threw it at Leo, and it flew so close to him that it nicked his left ear. Leo immediately stopped laughing. He frowned at Grace,

"What?" Grace glared at him. "Stop laughing. I may not have Olivia's aim, but that won't stop me from throwing this knife at your face," Leo, unlike last time did not laugh. The opposite, in fact, he looked hurt and rather sad.

"Grace. Why do you hate me so much?" Leo asked sadly. This question took Grace by surprise. She did not hate Leo and she had never meant to give off that impression.

"Well," Grace began slowly, weighing every word. "Even though I don't get along with you, hate is a strong word. I guess it's just oh, I don't... maybe a kind of protective kind of thing," Grace said truthfully.

"Over who? Emma?" Leo asked. Grace could feel Leo's curiosity mounting. So, she just told him all of it. Feelings, fears, memories, and secrets. (Well, not all her secrets. Secrets are secrets.) Everything, from the minute she heard the singing to that moment. Leo listened closely. As Grace continued to talk, Leo's eyebrow continued to get higher. Then, Leo told Grace his story.

"Well, I was born here in England. My mother, Annabelle was a maid for King George and Queen Evelyn, actually. Before Echidna came to Bodiam," He added quickly, at Grace's horrified expression. And my father, Henry worked at the local blacksmith," Grace noticed that when Leo talked about his father, his voice got bitter, from warm to cold in a matter of seconds. "My mother quit her job before she had me. That made it very difficult to keep our house and buy food. But somehow, my mother still managed to keep everyone fed, clothed, and happy. So, she thought. My father was not happy, not happy at all. He left my Mother and I like we were nothing. Like my mother hadn't loved, fed, cared, and let him live in her house for eight years," Leo growled. "After my father left, my Mother looked for a man to teach me how to fence. To distract me from the fact that my father had left us for some rich woman, not as beautiful, smart nor as kind as my Mother was. So, my Mother looked for a teacher, finally she found one. I went to the teacher often," Leo frowned. "Didn't know their name in the beginning. Never showed their face. Or talked much, for that matter. Only knew their eye color sapphire blue, lovely eye color. I assumed it was a bloke, because um, well er-" Leo blushed. Grace pursed her lips and furrowed her brows.

"Because of the skill, huh?" Grace finished coldly. Leo looked at feet.

"I, well no. Yes. So?" Leo said defensively. Grace nodded subtly.

"Think a person is a man, just because they're good with a sword. Have you met my friend, Emma?" Grace asked. Leo rolled his eyes slightly and shook his head.

"Ha ha. Very clever. Really amusing," Leo said sarcastically.

"What? It's the truth," Grace muttered, raising her eyebrows slightly.

"Do you want me to finish the story or not?" Leo asked seriously. Grace glared at him for a moment then, sighed.

"Fine," Grace snapped shortly.

"Thank you," Leo continued. "So, I kept going to the teacher. After a while my mother got very sick. I told the teacher that I would have to stop coming. They asked me about my mother, I told them what was wrong. My mother had tuberculosis, Grace. My teacher seemed very interested. I told them I would have to stop taking classes. They said it was fine. They gave me two free classes before I quit. The last class they revealed their identity. They were a woman, about my mother's age. Flaming red hair and crystal blue eyes. Looked a bit like you, actually. She told me her name was Rosemary. She had studied fencing her whole life. She had to leave my town. Gave me her sword," Leo finished, pulling out his sword and admiring it. "I took care of my mother for five months. My mother told me I needed to get a job. I started working for the General. Until one day, I came home and a bunch of doctors were at my house. My mother," Leo's voice broke. "Let's just say I've lived alone since that day," Grace wiped tears off her cheek and took a deep shuddering breath.

"Leo, I'm so sorry," Grace breathed.

"Oh, it's okay. Besides the sun is coming up. I'll look for a town around here," Leo managed a smile.

Grace had not realized the sun was rising until Leo had said it. She looked over her shoulder, and gasped. Behind the giant mountain, a blood red sun was coming up behind it. The clouds were tinged pink and orange; it truly was beautiful. Grace smiled feeling more peaceful and pleasant than ever. That's when Grace heard Emma scream.

CHAPTER 16

Grace whirled around, shocked. (Grace had gotten used to using her magic on their short ride.) Grace grabbed her bow out of midair and pulled the arrow clip out of her hair; she aimed the arrow in Emma's direction. Emma, Olivia, and Leo all stared at Grace. There was nothing around Emma.

"What happened?" Grace asked, lowering her bow slightly. Emma blushed.

"I was sleeping, and a branch brushed against me," Grace gaped at Emma, disbelievingly.

Finally, Grace spoke. "Sometimes, Emma, I forget you're a Princess," Grace said flatly. Everyone laughed. Olivia was glancing at a map, and Leo was sharpening his sword. Emma had pulled her hair out of its ponytail and was brushing it, humming softly. Olivia looked up from her map and put it back in the satchel hanging off her saddle.

"Let me guess, a five-hour ride from here," Leo sighed, sliding his sword back into its scabbard.

Olivia glanced at Leo. "No. Actually, there is a town really close to us," Olivia said, as if it was very obvious.

"Can I see the map?" Leo asked urgently. Olivia handed it to him. His eyes slid over it. He looked up, Grace saw a look of pure and absolute shock on his face.

"Leo? Are you okay?" Grace asked tentatively. Leo glanced at her. "We're going to my hometown," They rode for a few minutes, then, they reached the town. It was a lot bigger than Tunbridge. They got off their horses and tied them to a sturdy oak tree at the beginning of the town. A group of children were playing in the center of the town. Grace walked towards the group of children. They all looked at least a few years younger than Grace. The two children closest to Grace were girls. The younger sister looked like an exact replica of the older one. They had the same light blond hair in curls, icy blue eyes, and freckles across their small noses.

"ποιος είσαι?" the older girl asked.

"Ο πριγκίπισσα," Grace responded. Emma, Olivia, and Leo all looked confused. "What?" Grace demanded. Emma and Leo glanced at each other.

"You weren't speaking English, Grace," Olivia said shortly.

"But, I was- I mean, how would they have understood me?" Grace knew inside this was a foolish question but asked it anyway.

"We don't know, Grace. But, ask them where we can stay," Emma pointed out. While Grace asked the two children where they could stay, Emma, Olivia, and Leo discussed the plan. But not too far away.

"Lyla, send our best raven to Lady Artemis. She must be alerted at once that her daughter is here," said a girl's voice.

"Of course," The girl called Lyla said, walking away. The other girl looked up from her crystal ball, hazel eyes flaring.

"There are, apparently, no places for us to stay," Grace sighed, walking back to Emma, Olivia, and Leo. Emma sighed.

"Well, let's at least try to find some food and water," Olivia muttered. Everyone nodded their heads in agreement. They walked through the large town for a few minutes when Grace saw a piece of paper nailed to a store front. She snatched it off the door and read it again, astonished.

"Um, Leo? Before you left, did you do anything, oh, I don't know, dangerous and idiotic?" Grace asked, looking up from the piece of parchment and at Leo. Leo frowned slightly, but not like he was offended or annoyed, more like he was trying to remember. Ten hours ago, Leo would've said something sarcastic, but he didn't. Grace had sensed a changed between her and Leo ever since they had stayed up to dawn, talking. Emma and Olivia had indeed, looked at them strangely when Grace had asked Leo if he was okay. Leo's voice interrupted her thoughts.

"No. At least, I don't think so. Why?" Grace thrust the piece of paper at him, her head spinning. She watched Leo read. As he scanned it, he paled and his eyes widened. Emma snatched it out of his hands and began reading it aloud.

"Leo Smith, WANTED for thieving, denying authorities, and fleeing before trial," Emma, Olivia, and Grace all gaped at Leo.

"Leo," Olivia began slowly, "Did you do all these things?"

Leo looked up at her. "Yes,"

"Leo! Oh. My. Gods! You j-just happened not to tell us this?" Grace exclaimed, outraged.

"I'm sorry, I really am. I just prefer not to talk about my past-" Leo was cut off by a voice coming from the end of the street.

"Hey! You there! Leo Smith! You are under arrest!" The person that had yelled it was definitely sounded their age, maybe older. Olivia and Emma grabbed either of Leo's arms and ran. Grace followed, pulling the hood of her cloak on. She glanced back at the boy running after them, twenty men running behind him, armed. He had black hair and grey eyes. Then, at that moment, the boy and Grace locked eyes. Grace knew who the boy was Noah.

CHAPTER 17

As Grace ran, she wondered if she should keep running and keep her identity a secret or, take off her hood and talk to Noah. Her friends rounded a sharp corner and ran into a farmer's market. They stopped and hid behind a table.

"I know him. I know the boy, that's chasing us," Grace said quickly, trying to catch her breath. They all looked at her.

"And you just-just happened not to tell us this?" Leo exclaimed in a very good imitation of Grace's shocked voice. Grace glared at him. "Sorry," Leo muttered. Grace shot him an amused look.

"But, what? How? Help us!" Emma said, panicked, but curious.

"I met him at the ball. Do you remember, Emma? Black hair, grey eyes," Grace explained quickly, running behind the next table. Emma grinned.

"The boy that you talked to for most of the night, you mean," she said slyly. Grace blushed in spite of herself. Olivia cut in.

"Go talk to him. Bargain. We'll attack if absolutely necessary. But remember, we don't want a shootout. Go," Olivia nudged her out into the street. Grace walked out into the open. Noah pointed at her and all his men followed him. When they reached her, Grace walked forward and pulled back her hood. Grace watched Noah's jaw drop.

"Grace?" He asked weakly. Grace offered a small smile. "Noah?"

Noah put his hand up; his men lowered their firearms. Noah started walking towards Grace. All of the sudden, Noah fell to the ground. Behind him, silver eyes flaring, The General was holding his sword directly above Noah's unconscious body. Pure hatred and anger flooded through Grace's body as she locked eyes with The General. The General looked away and stabbed down. Grace summoned a sword as tall as she was. And, just before the tip of The General's sword sank into Noah's heart, Grace thrust out the sword and caught his sword with hers. Then, she pushed her sword up with all her might, getting The General's sword as far away from Noah as possible. Before The General could react, Grace drove her sword through The General's heart. Grace pulled the sword out of his heart and distantly heard the sword clatter to the ground. She heard The General's dying breath as if he was one hundred feet away. Her head was spinning. She had killed him, a person, a human just like her. What would Ella think? Even if he was cruel and harsh, he had loved her and she had loved him. Grace felt an arm wrap around her shoulders and guide her. Suddenly, Grace was falling to the ground. She hit the ground hard and then, everything went black.

CHAPTER 18

Grace woke up in a bed. She wished she was at home, in her bed. That is was all a dream, her mom, Hera, Echidna, all of it. But, she knew it wasn't. She had to stay strong for her kingdom, Emma, Olivia, her mom, and everyone. She sat up quickly and looked around. She was in a cell. It was a small room, with brick walls, cement floor and a tiny window about the size of a dinner plate, just big enough for arrows to come through, but also big enough for them to go out. Grace looked at the bed across from hers, there was someone in it. The figure rolled over and Grace realized it was Emma. She let out a sigh of relief and exhaustion. Then, Grace heard the sound of footsteps. Someone was coming towards them. Noah came into view. He was carrying Grace and Emma's sacks full of clothes. Noah was also struggling to carry a large plate of food. Grace bit back a laugh.

"Sleep alright?" He asked, setting down the platter of food.

"As good as you can for being in a cell of a friend's kingdom. Oh, and after you killed someone you knew for the first time," Grace crossed her legs and looked at Noah. "So, yeah, I slept great," She finished sarcastically. Noah frowned slightly, but didn't say anything. He whistled and a guard came around the corner. The guard gave him a small golden key. Noah took it out of the guard's hand and opened the cell door. He handed Grace's bag to her and, set Emma's bag down at the foot of her bed. The guard grabbed Noah's shoulder and pulled him away and out of the cell as if Grace and Emma were dangerous and mad. He then snatched the key out of Noah's hand and stalked away quickly. Once the guard's footsteps faded away, Noah turned to Grace.

"I'm sorry, Grace," Noah sighed, "Your friend Leo Smith must be hung. I'm so sorry, I wish there was something I could do," Grace thought about what Noah had said.

Maybe.."Noah," He looked at her, startled. "Um... there is something you could do," He raised his eyebrows.

"Anything," He responded.

Grace smiled at his trust. "It's nothing mad. Just one question," Noah seemed to relax slightly. "Do we get to watch Leo's hanging?" She finished. Noah looked surprised.

"I mean, yes. I can arrange it, I just assumed you didn't want to watch your friend hang," He replied, looking slightly uncomfortable.

"Yes, well, I do. When is it?" Grace asked brightly.

"One hour," Noah said, after looking down the hall at a clock. He jumped. "One hour?" He asked, his eyes widening. "Grace, I'm sorry, I have to go. Once you've changed, Oliver will walk you to the hanging," Noah muttered quickly, nodding to someone Grace thought was probably Oliver. Grace nodded and Noah strode away briskly. Grace got out of bed and walked the short distance of the cell to Emma's cot. Grace went to shake Emma awake, but before she could, Emma sat up, grinning. Her golden eyes were sparkling with amusement. Grace knew exactly what she was thinking and refused to ask about or discuss it.

"Well?" Emma asked, getting out of bed and walking over to the platter of food, still smiling like crazy.

"Well, what?" Grace exclaimed, feeling her face heat up.

Emma pulled on her shoes and looked up and Grace. She swallowed a mouthful of food "He's seems like a nice guy. And he likes you," Emma teased. Grace rolled her eyes.

"I'm so glad he's worthy of your approval," Grace said, feigning sincerity, shoveling food into her mouth.

"Grace, come on-" Emma was cut off by the sound of someone coming toward them. Grace glared at Emma, then turned to the door, annoyed. Oliver came around into their view. Grace nearly choked, and she heard Emma gasp then cover it up with a cough. Oliver was not much older than them, maybe fifteen or sixteen. He was very tan and had outdoorsy good looks. He had sandy brown hair and eyes, the eyes. The eyes of the wife of the man Grace had just killed. Ella's eyes.

CHAPTER 19

Grace was panicking inside. She wanted to scream and run. And sob uncontrollably, but instead, "Hello. You're Oliver, right?" She asked quickly, looking at Emma to silently tell her to act normal. Was Grace going crazy, or was this The General's and Ella's son? It's probably just some regular kid, with Ella's exact eye color, and fit what Ella had said about her son. Grace thought.

"Grace?" Grace had not realized someone was talking to her. Emma was staring at her. "Yes. I'm Oliver. You two are? Well, you're Grace," Oliver repeated, at least Grace thought he was probably repeating himself.

"I'm Emma and this is Grace," Emma replied, looking at Grace.

"Very well. I'll let you two freshen up and once you're ready, I'll walk you two to the hanging." Oliver walked away. Emma and Grace looked at each other. I know Grace mouthed, I'll talk to you about it after. Emma nodded. Okay. She mouthed back. The girls dressed in silence, both slightly in shock. They turned around at the same time. Grace was wearing a long sleeve black blouse and a long black skirt. Her black high heeled boots were uncomfortable, but they were the only shoes she had that seemed fit for the occasion. Emma was dressed in a short black velvet long sleeve dress with grey stockings and Grace's black flats. Emma tossed Graces' hairbrush at her and got her own out. Once both the girl's hair was brushed, Emma did a fancy braided bun on Grace's hair and then she put on Grace's black headband.

"Oliver?" Emma and Grace called at the same time.

"You two are ready?" Oliver asked tentatively, coming around the corner, but not looking into cell.

"Yes, thank you." Grace responded. Oliver unhooked the keyring from his belt and sifted through the keys quickly. He picked out a small silver key. Oliver opened the door and stepped back, allowing them to walk out.

"I'm terribly sorry but," He held up two pairs of handcuffs.

"That's alright, Oliver, you're just doing your job," Emma reassured him, holding out her hands. Oliver cuffed her hands, and then cuffed Grace's hands. He led them down the hall, past all the cells. Inside the cells were murders, thieves, and criminals alike. Grace shuddered as they passed, and could feel Emma shaking ever so slightly next to her. Grace knew why, Emma's family's castle had been attacked many times. They were soon joined by Olivia, she was also in handcuffs. Her chestnut hair was somehow curled and her eyes were filled with regret, sadness and anger. Usually, Grace thought of Olivia's eyes as a kaleidoscope of colors, but today they reminded her of shattered glass. Leo. Emma mouthed, as if that explained everything. But in a way, it did. There was something between Leo and Olivia, but they both remained somehow oblivious. They walked out of the dungeon and into the sunlight. Oliver led them over to a little space with three wooden chairs, there were two guards standing on either side of the chairs. Both the guards stood stiffly as if they had brooms tied to their backs. Oliver handed the guard facing him a piece of paper. The guard nodded and seized Emma's arm. Grace felt a spike of hot anger, she channeled that anger into magic. The guard yelped and let go of Emma. Emma stepped past him and sat down in one of the chairs like it was a throne. Grace smirked and sat down beside her. Grace didn't care if using this much magic could kill her, if anyone touched her best friend they were going to pay. Olivia looked like she was resisting the urge to smile. Grace barely saw her sit down, because she was so focused on the view in front of her. They were so close to the noose that Leo would probably see them out of the hundreds of people. Leo walked up to the noose, his hands tied and immediately spotted them in the crowd. His eyes sent Grace a frantic Help me or you better have a plan...

somewhere in between those two. Grace just smiled and waved, seeing as she already had a plan. His skin was very pale. Leo didn't smile back. Grace whispered the plan in Emma's ear, then Emma passed it on to Olivia. Grace nonchalantly materialized Emma and Olivia's weapons. The executioner wrapped the rope around Leo's neck and tightened it.

"I'll tell you when..." Grace whispered. The executioner walked over to the bar that dropped the trapped door, that Leo was currently standing on. "Wait," The people started cheering, the executioner tightened his grip on the bar, "Now!" Grace said, quietly but forcefully. Olivia hopped up and stabbed one of her knifes into the guard's neck, then pushed him to the ground retrieving her knife. Emma and Grace had jumped up at the same time as well. Emma had stood up and cut off the guard's head, while all of this was happening, Grace had shot an arrow at the executioner. It hit him right in between the eyes, Grace threw her bow up into the air and it disappeared. Behind Grace, Emma and, Olivia, someone snapped clearly and sharply. The sun tinged violet. The smell of fermented grapes filled the air. Chaos. Madness. Wood splintering, people screaming, minds snapping, the gallows ablaze. A person in a midnight blue cloak walked up to the gallows and pulled the bar down. Leo locked eyes with Grace as the trap door opened. The noose tightened on Leo's neck, and he dropped. Grace felt every muscle in her body tense. Grace couldn't breathe. Someone screamed, maybe it was her. Hot tears stung Grace's eyes. He can't be gone, no. Not like this, not killed like a criminal. The three girls stood there in shock.

"You three! Prisoners!" The King yelled. Grace saw someone else coming towards them, not a guard. A someone with sandy hair, and keys jangling on his belt.

"Come quickly, I can help you!" Oliver yelled, grabbing Grace's arm and running towards the doors to the castle.

CHAPTER 20

Grace ran. Grace ran and didn't look back. She wanted to stop and cry. Just sit and grieve, but she didn't. Tears were streaming down her face, and she could feel Olivia trying to pull against Oliver, trying to turn back. They reached the castle doors, and thundered down the halls. They turned a corner, and suddenly dozens of cloaked figures were standing in front of them. Grace, Emma, Olivia, and Oliver stood in a circle and got their weapons ready. One of the cloaked figures raised their hands and the world around Grace plunged into darkness, like a candle burning out. Grace awoke leaning against a wall. Her lungs felt like they were filled with ice. The minute she opened her eyes, tears were pouring out of them. Grace wiped away tears and looked around, then gasped. The cave was shimmering with thousands of gorgeous blue sapphires. There were cots in every corner of the cave, it had a tall domed ceiling. Nine to be exact. Across from Grace there was a wall lined with weapons. It seemed to give off the same energy as the bookcase had. Next to Grace were Olivia, Emma, and Oliver both unconscious.

"Misty, we cannot. We must give her the b-" Two people walked around the corner and stopped. Grace stood to face the strangers. It was two girls not much older than Grace, only thirteen or fourteen. One of the girls whistled and seven more girls came around the corner, all under fifteen. They were all wearing the same outfit. A short leather dress with knee length lace up sandals. And they each had a long piece of leather wrapped around each arm, wrapped from their bicep to their wrists. They also all had a different colored cloak fastened around their necks. The girl that had whistled stepped forward, she had long light brown curly hair, like she'd been walking on the beach for days. Her hazel eyes seemed silent and serene yet chaotic and lethal, like the ocean. But the one that shocked Grace about the girl was her cloak color. It was midnight blue. She had killed Leo.

"Who are you?" Grace snapped, the edge in her voice as sharp as a knife.

Leo's murderer looked at Grace. "I'm Misty and we're the Hunters of Artemis."

CHAPTER 21

"Wait-what?" Grace asked, thinking she misheard. Layla sighed.

"The Hunters of Artemis is a group of young women that roam around England, killing monsters and recruiting more maidens. When we find a maiden that wants to join, she pledges herself to Artemis and the Hunt. Then Artemis will make her immortal. If a hunter breaks her oath to foreswear romantic love forever, or if she falls in battle, she loses her immortality." Misty finished. Grace processed all this information.

"Okay, so you'll look thirteen or whatever age you are when you took oath, forever?" Misty nodded in agreement.

"I took my oath when I was thirteen, but that was one thousand years ago." Grace felt her eyes widen.

It was all so much for her to take in, her mom, Hera, Greek Mythology, monsters, the hunters. But, she had to stay strong for everyone, even if it killed her. Grace turned and faced Misty

"You killed Leo." Misty looked at Grace, a pitying look in her eyes.

"No, I didn't. Your friend is alive." Misty reassured, though her tone said, "Your friend is alive, sadly.".

"Where is he? What did you do to him?" Misty turned around and hissed at two of the girls in Greek. Grace knew she said, "Get the boy." The two girls walked back around the corner. They came back each holding one of Leo's arms. His hands were tied behind his back and he had a gag in his mouth. Leo looked incredibly disheveled. His dark hair was untidy, and his blue eyes looked hazy and out of focus. Grace noticed other details as well, all the scars on his arms were gone and his skin was no longer pale. Misty smiled and turned to the other hunters.

"Introduce yourselves. Tell Grace your name and godly parent. Show her the mark as well." Misty stepped aside and let the other girls step forward.

The first girl that walked up to Grace had raven color hair that reached her waist in a braid. Her vivid green eyes reminded Grace so much of Echidna, the way they seemed to shine with hatred and darkness. She had olive colored skin that contrasted beautifully with her green eyes.

"My name is Alexandrina, daughter of Hades." Her voice was full of so much pain and loss, Grace wanted to wrap her arms around her. And in between two pieces of leather she had a marking of a black skull and snake, that looked like it had been burned into her skin. Alexandrina's cloak was black.

The next girl walked up to her. She looked a lot like Grace, auburn hair in a bun, pale skin, and freckles. Her brown eyes seemed to shimmer with wisdom, as if she knew everything. "Amber, daughter of Athena." A grey owl was on her wrist, and her cloak was dark grey.

The next girl had blond hair like spun gold that cascaded to the middle of her back in perfect curls. Her dark lashes curled naturally over sparkling blue eyes and her cheeks were rosy. "Samantha, pleased to meet you, daughter of Aphrodite." Her voice was smooth and soft, almost like honey. Pink heart tattoo. Her peach colored skin seemed to glow under her rouge colored cloak.

Another girl walked up, her onyx hair fell to her shoulders, curled. The most startling thing about the girl was her eyes, they were the color of a hyacinth. "Violet, daughter of Dionysus, nice to meet you." Violet had tan skin that looked unusual but beautiful with her hair and eyes. She had a bunch of grapes burned into her skin and a cloak the color of a plum.

When the next girl walked up to Grace, Misty interjected. "This is my half-sister, Layla. We are both children of Poseidon." Grace could see how they were both children of Poseidon. Layla's eyes were a dazzling sea green and the green in Misty's hazel eyes were the exact same color. Her sleek brown hair had a small wave at the bottom of her hair.

Layla smiled at Grace. "I am so glad that I am one of the Hunters helping you on your quest." Layla's cloak was emerald green. The two daughters of Poseidon had the same sort of eerie calm hiding what Grace guessed was a storm of chaos and danger.

Three more to go, Grace thought. Grace was tired of getting greeted, and she didn't want to have to watch Emma, Olivia, and Oliver get introduced to all of these girls again. But, as the daughter of Artemis, it seemed rude not to meet her mother's followers.

The next girl walked up to Grace. Grace could sense something about this girl was different than the others. She carried herself differently, like she was expecting a fight to break out any minute. Her light ivory hair was in a perfect plait down her back. "Krisium. Ares." Her grey eyes were alert and her skin was the color of sand. Krisium was a hurricane of danger and destruction, and Grace could see it in her eyes. She had a red spear burned into her skin and a cloak the color of fresh blood.

The next girl had light brown hair that faded to blonde in a ponytail. Her eyes were blue and brown, a combination that Grace had never seen. On her bronze skin, was a blue lightning bolt. "Selene, daughter of Zeus." Her voice was fast but calm, and her cloak was royal blue.

The last girl stepped forward. Her charcoal hair was down and wavy, but had a braided crown. Her bright grey eyes were a painful reminder of the General. Grace looked at Oliver, uncomfortable. "I'm Vanessa, daughter of Hecate." Her tattoo was of two torches, crossed which shone deep purple against her pale skin.

"Vanessa is the one who's magic made it uh..easier to bring you to our hideout." Misty explained, hesitating before saying easier. "Now Grace, it is time for you to meet our leader, Zöe, daughter of Zeus."

CHAPTER 22

When the last girl walked around the corner, Grace immediately knew this was the leader, even without Misty telling her. Her ebony hair was pulled back in an impeccable braid that fell all the way to her thighs and she had a simple silver circlet on top of her head. She had electric blue eyes and pale skin.

"Grace Evans. It is my pleasure to meet you. I assume Misty told you everything." She had a very strong British accent.

"Yes, she has." Grace responded.

Zöe had a blue lightning bolt on her wrist along with a bracelet with a crescent moon on it. It wasn't just the circlet that told Grace Zöe was the leader. It was the way that she held herself and walked. She walked like a queen, and the other girl's heads bowed slightly when she walked past. She didn't have to try to be perfect, like Grace had to. She was meant to be a leader.

"I see you are traveling with a male." Zöe remarked coldly, saying the word male as if she hadn't ever been more disgusted.

"Yes. We are." Grace snapped, offended that Zöe was talking about Leo like that.

Zöe smiled, raising her eyebrows slightly. "You have fire in your eyes, Child of Artemis." Grace tried to have less fire in her eyes. "Do not try to hide it. That is what I look for in maidens to join the Hunt. A certain edge. A certain air. And you have it."

Grace didn't say anything. She didn't know what to say. Grace heard rustling behind her, and turned around, happy to have a reason to look away from Zöe and the Hunters. Emma, Olivia, and Oliver were awake.

The rest simply blurred together, Olivia shouting at the Hunters about Leo, Emma stepping in before Krisium and Olivia started fighting, the Hunters introducing themselves, and Leo waking up. Grace paid more attention after Leo woke up. Olivia hugged him and wouldn't let go, Leo and Olivia somehow communicating without talking. Emma and Samantha both smiled. Everything started calming down, and Grace tuned out again.

"Let's eat." Misty said, breaking the silence. The Hunters fed Grace, Emma, Leo, Olivia, and Oliver well.

Grace realized there was a small square of something golden brown that looked like a delicacy Grace had loved when she was a child, she also realized that Emma, Olivia, Oliver, and Leo didn't have any, but all the Hunters did. There was one more strange thing she had that no one else had (except the Hunters). A small bottle of iridescent goldish liquid. The liquid was pretty, and both things looked appetizing, still, she hesitated.

"What are these?" Grace asked loudly, to no one in particular.

"Ambrosia and nectar. The food and drinks of the gods." Zöe responded.

"But, why do we eat the food of the gods? We're not gods. Are we?" Grace asked hesitantly.

Zöe laughed. "No, Grace. But, demigods can have a tiny bit of the food of the gods. Remember Grace, too much will kill you."

Grace slowly took a bite of the thing Zöe had called ambrosia. Warmth spread from Grace's fingertips to her feet. It tasted just like the creamy lemon custard her mom made so often. Emma and Grace had eaten it on one of their sleepovers when they were 9. Grace opened her eyes slowly. Then, out of nowhere, there was a knock.

CHAPTER 23

The loud knock was followed by a shout. "Open up! You are under arrest for treason!"

The Hunters, Emma, Olivia, Leo, Oliver, and Grace all stood up, weapons at the ready.

"You have ten seconds before we blow you out of there!" The voice yelled.

Zöe gestured to everyone and hissed in Greek, but which Grace understood easily. She had said, "Follow me. Quickly." Grace glanced at the door. They all started running out of the cave. Zöe insured every Hunter got out safely. Even though Zöe seemed cold and commanding, she cared very much about the Hunters. After all, they were her family. The ground shook and Grace was blown off her feet. Grace braced herself for hitting the ground. Instead, she felt as if she had landed on hundreds of pillows. That didn't stop the ringing in her ears and the wave of nausea that rolled over her, as they cave doorway behind her blew to pieces. At least fifty guards swarmed the doorway, archers in the front. "Shields at the ready!" Zöe yelled.

Grace hit the floor as arrows imbedded themselves in the shields of the Hunters. She rolled over and knocked an arrow in her bow. Just as she was about to shoot, at least a dozen spears flew over her head. Grace watched them as several guards fell. Grace realized they weren't spears, they were hardened wine! Blasts of purple shot at at the guards. Skeletons burst out of the ground, attacking the guards. A cyclone of water splashed over a group of shoulders. Grace saw Misty's eyes narrow as she prepared to strike again. They're using their powers. Grace thought. They were so skilled and trained, using their powers with precision and ease. Grace wondered why she didn't learn how to control her powers from the Hunters. As a team, the Hunter's worked to defeat many of the soldiers, but they kept coming.

"They won't stop!" Grace yelled to Zöe. "We need to clog the entrance." She nodded and advanced. Grace and Zöe advanced with their bows. All the archers were dead, so the rest of the guards had swords. Zöe and Grace ran towards the guards, Hunters, Olivia, Emma, and Oliver all behind them. The guards ran to meet them. Several Hunters had climbed onto ledges in the cave, and were shooting at the guards with their bows and arrows. Hunters that had swords, spears, and knives rushed into combat, slashing, stabbing, and throwing spears. Grace killed. Ruthlessly. Quickly.

Still, Grace was nothing compared to Emma. Emma was fighting with the same ferocity Grace had seen when the guards at Echidna's castle had attacked. The charismatic twinkle in her eyes had vanished, replaced by a fiery intensity. Her usual warm grin had transformed into a dark scowl. Guards fell at her feet, each death gorier than the other. Blood covered Emma. Grace expected her to look solemn, or even show a bit of remorse. There was no remorse in Emma's expression. Simply a cold mask of hatred. For once, Grace felt scared of her best friend. What is wrong with me? Grace scolded herself. Emma is my best friend. She would never hurt me. Grace took a deep breath, turning her bow into her two hunting knives. Grace glanced wearily at Emma one more time. And as Grace watched Emma, time seemed to slow down. A guard was standing behind Emma, sword poised to run her through. Grace instantly paled. She began running towards her best friend, shouting her name. Emma whipped around to the sound of Grace's voice. The guard thrust out his sword just as Emma turned to face him. Grace didn't reach her in time. The guard buried his sword deep into Emma's gut.

CHAPTER 24

Emma's eyes widened in shock, choking. Grace ran. Like she had never ran before. She tore across the battlefield, too focused on Emma to remember the plan she and Zöe had come up with. Grace wanted to kill him. This man. She didn't care if he had children, a wife, or was the King's favorite guard. He had harmed Emma, her best friend since Grace could remember. And he would pay dearly for it. She saw many fall, but none of that mattered. Emma's killer was only feet away. Grace wanted to watch him bleed, she wanted to plunge her knife deep into his head. To watch him take his last breath. Before she knew it, she was stabbing the man repeatedly, and slashing at his heart. Grace felt no sympathy. No remorse. She felt like this man had destroyed world. Grace suddenly realized the battle raging around her had stopped. Hunters and guards alike and stopped and watched as Grace murdered a man in cold blood, because he had stabbed her best friend. She finally stopped slashing and stabbing, covered in more blood than Emma. Grace, her addrenilen gone, fell to her knees. She turned to Emma, her golden hair flecked with sweat and blood fanned out behind her.

"Oh, Emma," Grace sobbed. The anger had disappeared from Emma's eyes. In fact, everything had disappeared from her eyes. The light, the warmth, the sparkle, the life. All gone. Tears streamed off of Emma's cheeks and into her hair, putting streak marks through the blood flecked on her face. That's how Grace knew Emma was in pain. Tears. Emma cried a lot, she was very emotional. But she never cried because of pain. For a minute, Emma tried to steady her breathing, and Grace could tell she was fighting. Then, something clicked inside of Emma, or that's what it looked like to Grace. Her expression melted from tense pain to a soft, peaceful look. Emma's entire body seemed to slacken, relax. She didn't look like she was going to die, just as if she was going to take a short nap, and that she and Grace would see each other soon. This just made Grace more grief stricken. Grace felt tears sting her eyes. Emma just smiled softly, not looking pained at all anymore. Grace sobbed harder, pressure building up in her chest. Emma just continued staring calmly at her. Grace couldn't understand why Emma seemed so calm, suddenly, she realized why. Emma was not afraid. No fear of flying. No fear of leaving.

She had said it before, when they were 10. She and Grace had just snuck up to the tallest spire and were laying on the flat top, watching the stars. Grace asked, "Are you afraid of dying?" Emma was silent for a long minute.

"No," She had responded simply. Grace winced, for a cold hand had reached out, grasping hers. It was Emma's. Usually, Emma's touch comforted Grace. Her faint vanilla scent as if she walked through fields of vanilla flowers in her spare time. Her gentle, warm touch. Her clear, honest copper eyes, flecked with green and dark brown. Grace was brought back to reality by those very eyes. Grace realized that Emma was trying to say something. Grace leaned down, and Emma's lips grazing her ear. Since Grace always thought of Emma as her anchor to the world, and so strong, she imagined her to sound strong and ready to rush back into battle.

Grace had never heard Emma's voice so weak and frail. "Find Chiron." Somewhere deep down inside, Grace knew this was it, the end. Emma was about to die.

CHAPTER 25

Emma's breathing had become shallow, her eyes sliding in and out of focus. Grace realized the hardest thing in the world was watching someone you love die slowly. All of the guards were dead, but Hunters did not step forward to help. Grace knew why, but it still made her mad. Emma's wound was beyond repair. No medicine. No magic. Grace looked and the sword, buried to the hilt in Emma's stomach. When Grace thought Leo had died, she felt like she had fallen from a spire, all the air knocked from her chest, her head spinning. Emma dying was a thousand times worse. Grace couldn't remember what day it was, where she was, or even who she was, just that she didn't want Emma to die. Grace started convulsing slightly, her head throbbing so hard, she couldn't see. Grace was shaking. Grace felt like she was broken. Something inside of her was broken. She felt fragile. Weak. Hollow.

"Stay with me, Emma, please," Grace pleaded, sobbing into Emma's chest. Her hands were slick with Emma's and guards blood. Tears flooded out of her eyes and down her shirt. Grace tried to wipe away tears but only smeared her face with Emma's blood. Tears and blood soaked Grace, and she could taste the blood and salty tears fill her mouth. Emma's eyes fluttered. She stared at Grace, clearly pained to see Grace like this, crazy but weak. "Please, stay with me," Grace sobbed so hard she couldn't breathe.

"Always," Emma muttered, barely audible. Emma stared into Grace's eyes. Her eyes glazed over, her skin paled. Her grip slackened on Grace's hand and she didn't move again. Grace's heart shattered into a million pieces. She did not feel like crying. She did not feel like moving. She did not feel like breathing. She did not want to feel, so she didn't. She sat, holding Emma's hand, eyes glued on something in the distance that wasn't there. She wanted to sit by Emma's side until she starved or froze. Someone grabbed Grace from behind, but Grace would not let go. She screamed and kicked until the person left. Grace didn't care who it was or what they wanted. Anyone that touched Grace, or even talked to her, either left after a few seconds trying to pry her from Emma's body and failing, or failing but also walking away with an injury. Grace didn't know how long she sat there, holding Emma's hand and staring, and occasionally screaming at someone if they looked at her. She watched the sun set and rise over and over. Then, she realized she had been moved. By magic, obviously, because no one would touch her. Grace didn't care where she was, or if she was in danger. Days passed, but Grace didn't move, wishing to have Emma back.

CHAPTER 26

Grace opens her eyes. She's in her bedroom, except she was not. Everything is white, like the room had all the color sucked out of it. Grace still found it calming. Seeing her bed, smelling her favorite rain and jasmine candle, the faint smell of her mother, like freshly baked cookies and pine needles, the view of the archery range out her window. Everything seemed to be hazy, light, blurry even though somehow dreamy and beautiful. It seemed to be lit by a light that wasn't there. Maybe I'm dead, Grace thought, walking over to her desk. Most people would be sad, scared even, but Grace felt elated. I get to see Emma again, as if on cue, Grace heard someone approaching behind her. She immediately knew it was Emma. The warm hand grasping her shoulder, the smell of vanilla that somehow overpowers everything, though it is so faint. "Grace," Emma said, her voice soft. Grace allowed Emma's voice to fill her up, flow through her mind and body, and wrap herself in the warmth. Grace turned around. Emma was standing in front of her, the unearthly glow encasing her body. Emma was wearing a simple white silk dress, with thin straps, the neckline in the shape of a v. It fell just past her knees, and her hickory colored hair fell down to her shoulders in a smooth curtain. She looked different. Her caramel colored eyes were still warm, but now tinged with pain. Her hair seemed darker, and her skin seemed paler.

"I'm so sorry." Grace said.

Emma smiled gently. "Grace, no need to be sorry. This isn't your fault." Emma's hand grabbed Grace's. It felt so real, Grace smiled. Then, Grace felt a change. The soft light brightened, Emma's grasp loosened, the room faded away. Emma just looked at Grace calmly and her soothed with honeyed words, "Just remember-" The room disappeared completely.

Strangely, even once the room was completely gone, Grace still felt a warm hand gripping hers. Grace's eyes flew open and she was about to rip her hand away when she saw it was Olivia. Grace extracted her hand less aggressively, but pulled away nonetheless. Olivia didn't pay any mind to the fact Grace didn't want to talk or move or receive any sympathy. Olivia pulled Grace into her arms. At first, Grace was stiff and tense, since she had gone so long without anyone touching her. Then slowly, very slowly, Grace relaxed and gave into the hug. Olivia's arms were warm and comforting. Grace wanted to stay in Olivia's arms forever, where no one could see her tears, no one could talk to her. Grace tried to steady herself, but just when she thought her breathing was back to normal, the tears began. Grace had only seen Olivia act like this once, when Emma had gotten stabbed in the shoulder. Just thinking about Emma made Grace sob harder, losing her train of thoughts. Olivia rarely showed the side of herself that was caring, and motherly. That caring, motherly, and sweet side of her was usually masked by the young fierce warrior. Grace expected Olivia to smell like Emma, warm, sweet. Instead, when Grace wrapped herself in Olivia's arms she was greeted by a smell that seemed like a mixture of cinnamon and citrus. It was an unexpected combination, but it worked, the spice and warmth of the cinnamon, the sour and sweet of the citrus reflected her ever changing personality. Olivia started crying, almost as hard as Grace. "I am so sorry Grace," Olivia muttered into Grace's ear. Grace pulled away instinctively. Olivia nodded with understanding.

"When my parents died, I didn't want condolences, I just wanted someone to be there. Of course, no one was there. I don't want that to happen to you Grace." Grace felt guilty. Olivia didn't need to keep talking, they both knew where she was after her parents died. All this time, Grace didn't want to talk to anyone, when Olivia understood what she was going through. Maybe even better than Grace did herself. And Olivia had had ten times worse, with no one. All alone in the damp, dark cell Emma and Grace had found her in. The day Emma and Grace had found Olivia felt like years ago, which it could have been, for all Grace knew. She could have been sitting by Emma's body for an hour or a thousand years.

CHAPTER 27

After Samantha had used "charmspeak" as the Hunters called it, on Grace and drinking a potion that allowed her to have dreamless sleep, Grace had finally collected herself. If you count collecting yourself as not bursting out crying for no reason, or blacking out. Grace saw that she was back in the Hunters' cave. None of the Hunters Grace saw fall were dead, just injured. Zöe explained that after Emma died, more guards had arrived but that Grace had subconsciously used her magic to kill all the guards. Oh, I didn't attack Olivia, Leo, or any of the Hunters, it was a guard that grabbed me. And I wasn't just screaming, I was using magic. Grace thought. She was glad she hadn't hurt any of the Hunters or her friends. Zöe continued talking. She said that they had moved Emma's body and Grace to the cave by using magic. Grace only heard the last part. Emma's body was here. In a cave. Zöe seemed to read Grace's mind.

"We used magic to preserve her body, she's over there." Zöe muttered. Grace was surprised to see the pain in her face. Zöe smiled dryly. "Grace, I care. I care about what happens to every maiden. Emma was incredibly brave, don't think she died for nothing. She knew you could reach Chiron and was willing to sacrifice herself... for you. She made that choice when she followed you to the singing voice, the cave, Hera. Any other person would have backed out long ago, yet, she didn't. She knew the possibilities, she accepted them. She loved you Grace. Don't forget it." Grace was yanked back in time, to the time when her mother's letter said, I love you so much, never forget it. More promises. Promises to be broken. Grace felt her grip on reality slipping. She dug her fingernails into her palms. Grace stood up, and walked over to Emma's body. Emma looked the same way she did in Grace's dream. The white dress, the hair, the slightly paler skin. Grace drew in a rattling breath, attempting to stay calm, collected. She fell to her knees and began weeping. Grace turned her sadness to magic, using the magic to fashion a small knife, and poking herself with it on her wrist. She gasped in pain, but the effect was immediate, she wiped away the tears and stood. She felt someone walk up behind her. It was Zöe. Zöe stepped closer to Emma's body and took a deep breath. Grace was confused, what was Zöe going to do? Zöe raised her hands a few inches above Emma's body. If anyone else started doing this, Grace would attack them, but Grace trusted Zöe, and Zöe knew what she was doing. Misty seemed to know what Zöe was doing as well, because she launched to her feet. Misty began talking, her voice rushed, looking anxious, scared even.

"Zöe, the sacrifice for this spell is far beyond what we have-" Zöe cut her off, "I am well aware of the risk, Misty." Misty stepped back, looking embarrassed, but still frightened. Zöe looked back at Emma. Electricity crackled at Zöe's fingertips, her vibrant blue eyes flashed blank white for a split second, then they returned to their normal color. All the color drained from her pale skin, and the electricity on her fingertips formed into thin ropes of pure energy. These electric cables wrapped around Emma's lifeless body, and Emma's skin became almost transparent, and Grace could see the electricity flowing through her body. By now, Grace was getting more and more worried about what Zöe was doing. She looked weaker every second. And not just physically, Grace felt like something was happening to her inside. Zöe's vivid cerulean eyes had faded to a murky saxe blue. Her face had turned white as snow, tinged with grey and green. Zöe was shaking so badly Grace wondered how she kept doing magic. Grace turned around. Misty locked eyes with her. Suddenly, Grace felt Misty in her head. She could just feel her presence. What Zöe is about to do will kill her. You must help her. How? Channel your magic into Emma's body. Be ready to die bringing Emma back. Be willing to sacrifice everything. And use those emotions to bring Emma back. Don't break away. Keep channeling your magic, no matter the amount of pain. Please try. Zöe will die. I'll try. I promise. Grace felt Misty leave. She turned her attention to Emma. She remembered what Misty had told her. Be willing to give everything. And Grace was. She channeled every emotion she could muster, sadness, happiness, fright, emptiness, pain, nostalgia, and anger, until she conjured thin silver strands that wrapped around Emma. The pain came as fast as thought, it was unimaginable, but remembering Misty's words, Grace didn't break the connection. No sight, no sound, no feeling except for pain. Every muscle in Grace's body felt like they were burning, her blood turned to fire, and it felt all her bones were disintegrating. Before she had done the magic, she had felt many things, now she only felt one thing. Agony. Grace wanted to scream in pain, but no sound came out of her mouth. It felt like the weight of the world was crushing her, Grace wanted to black out, but the pain was so intense it made her hold on. Her vision turned fuzzy, and everything tinged red. Dead, but not allowed to die, alive, but as good as dead. The pain was all she felt. Then, just as quickly as it had came, the agony melted away, until she only felt the smallest amount of pain. If Grace had been on the line in between life and death, she had gently shifted to the side that was life. She no longer felt the pain that had been unbearable seconds ago, and could breathe again.

It took Grace a few seconds to realize what happened. Zöe lay on the ground at Grace's feet, and she was breathing shallowly. Grace looked at Emma. Surely after all the magic and pain Grace and Zöe endured, Emma was alive. Instead, Emma didn't move at all. Grace stood for what felt like forever, but Emma still didn't move. It didn't work.

CHAPTER 28

Grace head started throbbing, and she was in more pain than she was doing the magic to bring Emma back. Tearing her eyes away from Emma's lifeless form, she knelt at Zöe's side. Zöe's eyes were clouded, as if she was already somewhere far away. Misty was also kneeling by her side, silent tears running down her cheeks. Zöe looked away from Misty, who now looked like she was hyperventilating. Grace and Zöe locked eyes.

"Grace. It has been a pleasure helping you." Zöe nodded, her royal blue eyes were clear and surprisingly warm. Grace started crying. Zöe was thousands of years old, dying now, to save Grace's best friend. And that hadn't even worked. Looking into her warm eyes, Grace cried even harder, reminded of Clara and home. If Grace hadn't been so foolish and followed Hera's voice, Emma would be alive and Zöe would have lived for who knows how much longer. She would have woken up, gone hunting, and everything would be normal. Instead, she had been arrogant by trying to find out what the singing was, and then thought she would just have a normal life after that. And didn't that go well. Grace held Zöe's hand as she tried to speak.

"I tried." She managed to say with a strained breath. "But.. but don't let us die in vain." Zöe removed her circlet and handed it to Grace.

"Zöe, I can't take this." Grace pleaded, tears shining. "I brought this on everyone. I don't deserve it."

Zöe with a small, soft laugh, pressed it into Grace's hand. "Hold onto this remember me by...good luck...sister." with that Zöe took one last breath. Misty started to shake rapidly in the corner mumbling to herself. Grace felt as if every rational thought and emotion was ripped from her, and everyone's voices were simply static, their forms blurry. The rest was simply a flash. The Hunters deciding who would take Zöe's place, getting transported by magic to the horses, riding far away from the castle. While they were riding, Grace looked over at Oliver, deciding to tell him about his parents.

"Oliver. I-I have something to tell you. I knew your father and mother." Oliver paled so quickly, Grace was afraid he might faint.

"You did?" He asked, his voice brittle and thin.

"Yes." Grace responded cautiously.

"Where are they?" He asked, his voice hardening.

"Well, your mother is living at the Jones castle. And your father..." Grace trailed off.

"What about him, Grace?" Oliver snapped, his voice harsh.

Grace could swear her voice dropped an octave lower when she spoke. "He's dead."

Oliver's face softened to shock, then turned stone cold with anger. Fury blazed in his eyes, a hatred so deep and dark, Grace felt scared. "Who killed him?" Oliver demanded, his voice shaking with anger.

Grace's head swam. What if this happened to her? If she had never met her parents, then found out one of them was dead. She would be absolutely furious, and if Oliver said he had killed her father... Grace would surely take out her anger and grief on him.

"Who killed him?" Oliver asked again, the fury in his voice making Grace shirk away.

"I did." Grace said quietly. This apparently sent Oliver over the edge. He was completely unhinged. Oliver drew his sword on Grace. Grace could have easily disarmed and killed him, if she wasn't still mourning Emma and Zöe, and feeling so guilty for what she did to the General. Hot nausea ripped through Grace's stomach. Her head swam and she could feel herself swaying slightly. Oliver stabbed out with his sword, knocking her off of her horse, and cutting a deep gash in her cheek. Grace laid on the ground, holding her throbbing cheek. She heard Oliver jump off of his horse, his footsteps coming towards her. Grace curled into a tighter ball, waiting for death. It never came. She heard Oliver come near her, saw him raise his sword above her limp figure. He stabbed downward, only to have his blade caught by another, Misty. Then, just as Grace had killed Oliver's father, Misty killed Oliver. He hit the ground, and Grace crawled over to him. She didn't care if he stabbed her again, she deserved it. He looked into her eyes, the pain in them making her gut wrench. Oliver beckoned Grace, and she leaned in closer to his lips. "I just wanted to meet my parents. Don't let this happen to any of the others. Mine should be the last death. Please..." His eyes closed. Grace shivered. It sent an eerie chill up her spine, what Oliver had said. She knew she had to ensure it. His would be the last death. Grace made a silent promise to Oliver as she conjured flowers, to lay on the dirt mound she had made. Grace stood up and walked away, not looking back. She did not cry, she simply looked up and said goodbye.

Remounting her horse, Grace laid her head on Rose's neck and fell asleep. They finally stopped in a breathtaking part of the forest. With it's beautiful emerald green pines and cambridge blue skies, it seemed to be mocking Grace. The Hunters set up camp with astonishing speed. Grace got to stay in the biggest tent with Misty, Leo, and Olivia. Misty definitely looked different from when Grace had first met her. Her gold and brown flecked eyes were red and puffy from crying, and her rich olive skin had lost it's shimmer and glow, turning it a dull pale and sickly green. As for Olivia and Leo, they looked the same. They kept shooting each other shifty looks, an odd look on their faces. Sadness, guilt, and longing clouded their eyes when they looked at each other. Emma had been right, there was something between those two.

"Misty," Grace said, surprised by how weak and broken her voice sounded. "You should get some sleep. Don't worry." There was another lie.

Misty pursed her lips, then her shoulders slumped. "Very well."

The sun started setting and Grace went outside the tent to watch it. Leo and Olivia joined her. As the sun set, Grace cried. She didn't cry loudly, she didn't cry for attention. She just cried. Leo and Olivia noticed after a while, and wrapped their arms around her. Grace was glad for their warmth. They didn't speak, they just sat and watched the sunset, mourning for Emma and Zöe.

CHAPTER 29

When the sun had fully set, Grace was still sitting in the exact same spot, without Olivia and Leo. They had left at least an hour ago, asking if she wanted them to stay. She wanted to scream at them, Of course I want you to stay! My best friend just died as well as my mother's most devoted follower! Please stay. Instead, she had just smiled and waved them off, telling them she'd be fine. Lies. Tears blinded Grace's eyes. She was a liar. Not just small ones like these, ones like allowing Emma to come with her on the night of her thirteenth birthday. Telling her it would be fine, then getting her killed. Horrible thoughts swirled in Grace's mind, until she simply closed her eyes and fell asleep. Grace had a dream that she was in a cold dark cell, not much different than Echidna's. She was shackled to a bed, the chains cutting into her wrists, rubbing them raw. Grace felt like she had just died, her head throbbing, her heart pounding. Her throat was dry, and she hadn't eaten for more than a day, feeling her energy slipping away. Through the slot in her metal door, a bowl of water, like a dog bowl, clanged to the ground, spilling half of it in the process. She crawled off of the bed, to the bowl of water, expecting to see her own reflection, only to see two golden eyes glaring back at her. Not her eyes. Emma's eyes. Grace woke up screaming, she sat bolt right up. It was not even morning yet, the crisp air biting at Grace. Everyone burst out of their tents, weapons drawn. Misty lowered her bow and surged forward, concern etched on her face.

"Grace, what happened?" She asked, Misty's voice was tight and rigid.

"Uh, bad dream." Grace blushed, realizing it was a stupid announcement.

She was the daughter of Artemis, not some prissy and shrill child. Grace expected everyone to be annoyed at her, instead, Misty looked even more worried. A few of the Hunters shifted uncomfortably, only Olivia and Leo looked confused.

"What did you see?" Misty said softly, her tone dead serious.

"Emma, she was trapped somewhere, in a cave, and alive." Grace responded.

Misty addressed Grace and the Hunters in Greek. Grace translated easily,

"We have to go." She told Olivia and Leo what Misty had said. By the time they had all mounted their horses, the Hunters had broken down camp. Misty climbed onto her all black horse, it's sea green eyes flaying anyone that stepped in its path. A soft voice whispered in Grace's mind. Grace rode in front of Misty and her horse.

"Misty, no." Misty's eyebrows raised. "I'm meant to do this alone, it's my fault," Grace's voice was steady and assured, very different from her voice last night. Misty looked at her, searching Grace. After a long second, her face relaxed.

"Alex, pick four Hunters to go with you. I will protect and lead Grace to Chiron with my group, and you will take yours and find a new hideout." Misty sounded gentle, but firm.

Alexandrina, the daughter of Hades, looked surprised.

"Misty, I want to help you-" Misty cut her off, "I am lieutenant. Am I not?" Misty snapped, the gentleness in her voice replaced by a cold anger. Alex nodded. "Yes, lieutenant." "Do as Zöe would do." Alexandrina grabbed a few Hunters, Layla, the other daughter of Poseidon, Krisium, the grey eyed daughter of Ares, and Selene, Zöe's half sister, and melted into the shadows. The remaining Hunters, Amber, the daughter of Athena, Samantha, the ravishing daughter of Aphrodite, Violet, the daughter of Dionysus who made everyone temporarily mad during Leo's hanging, and Vanessa, the daughter of Hecate who had brought Olivia, Leo, Grace, and Oliver to the cave, including Misty, hopped on their horses. "Olivia, Leo, come." Misty said. Grace hugged Olivia and Leo. Misty slid off her horse and hugged Grace, then straightened Grace's diadem. Misty leapt back on her horse, smiling. She spurred her horse Anaklusmos, then, like the tide it was named after, she and Grace's friends were swept away. A wave of sadness rolled over Grace, and she felt more alone than ever. She mounted Lilac, and even though Emma had been captured, she was alive. At first, Grace thought Zöe had died for nothing, but now she realizes, Zöe had risked life because she believed Grace could find Chiron. So did Emma. Grace flicked Lilac's reigns, and they sped off in the dark, headed for the castle of the boy with grey eyes.

CHAPTER 30

By the time she reached Noah's castle, the sun was barely rising over the mountains. Grace threw open the doors of the castle to see a tall man with an air of superiority. He opened his mouth to say something, Grace ripped an arrow through his heart. She stormed through the doors, stepping on the man's arm as she passed. If she saw anyone that wasn't the King, Queen, or Noah, Grace would shoot or stab them quickly and easily. She knew it was rude and unfair, they hadn't killed Emma or Zöe. She also frankly didn't care. Finally, she reached the Throne Room. After pushing through the doors aggressively, and taking out six guards, she glared around the room, catching her breath. If Grace wasn't so angry, with the adrenaline pumping through her veins, and the shrill ringing in her ears, she may have actually enjoyed the room. It had deep blue walls, lined with many photos, framed by gold, which contrasted beautifully with gilded thrones. Grace caught a glance of herself, and felt herself not able to look away. Her auburn hair was flowing over her shoulders, making it look like fire. Zöe's circlet was braided into her hair, which was pulled back, but only two thick strands, not all of it. She also had two small strands of red hair in front of the circlet. She guessed Misty or Olivia had done that sometime after Zöe died. Grace felt surprised by the wild, empty look in her eyes, like a caged animal. Her borrowed cloak had been shredded by trees and swords, it was also stained red with blood. She suddenly felt scared of herself, scared because of how much her looks had changed. Sure, she certainly didn't feel like the same girl she was on her thirteenth birthday. She couldn't imagine what everyone else thought of her. Grace tore her eyes away from the mirror, and continued looking around. There were four thrones, the largest and tallest in the middle, which belonged to the King, one just off to the side, nearly as tall, for the Queen, then there were two, one slightly taller than the other. Grace knew one was for Noah's brother, Ethan, and the other for Noah, himself. Just above their thrones were a family photo. Noah's father had ebony hair that matched Noah's exactly, and dark brown eyes that twinkled with mischief, his father was wearing a regal blue and gold king's suit, with a jeweled sword hanging at his side. Noah's mother, on the other hand, had lustrous blonde locks that tumbled down to her shoulders in loose curls, and light grey eyes like Noah's. She was beautiful in a regal yet warm and interesting sort of way, that made you want to bow, but also want to have tea with her. Noah's brother was quite handsome, though he did not have Noah's playful smile and charming twinkle in his eyes. He instead had a cold and regal glint in his dark eyes, like coffee without the warmth, like his mother, though without the kindness. His sepia brown hair was close cropped, and his chiseled jaw and high cheekbones made him look like a cold and creepy statue, one that you admired but feared, and could never grow close to. Noah looked exactly liked Grace had remembered, simply younger and had a happier blissful sort of smile, one that Grace guessed had gone away once Ethan had died.

"Twenty guards, five butlers, and a steward, all dead. And to be killed by no other than Grace Evans, princess of England." Someone said behind Grace, their voice a teasing drawl. Grace turned and saw present day Noah, leaning against the wall. He smiled wryly. "Let's go for a walk, Princess." Noah's slate colored eyes studied Grace as they walked, making her shift uncomfortably. Noah had led her to the most breathtaking garden Grace had ever seen. It had thousands of bushes and trees, all blossoming with gorgeous flowers. Beautiful fountains, adorned with stone statues and small birds, stone benches under stunning arches of marble. They stopped at a lovely archway that had marble vines wrapped around it, with rose trees growing on either side of it. Finally, Grace had to break the thick silence,

"Ακούστε, Νώε, λυπάμαι πραγματικά γι 'αυτούς τους ανθρώπους στο κάστρο σου." As soon as Grace said it, she knew it had been Greek.

Apparently, Noah didn't. "Pardon? What did you say? That didn't sound like English." Noah insisted, his eyes narrowing in suspicion.

"Nothing." Grace snapped quickly, then blushed. "Sorry, that was rude. Never mind." Noah smirked. She kills over twenty people and now she's apologizing for being rude. Wow. She knew he was teasing her, but somehow, it didn't seem mean. Grace still glared at him. "Where's Emma?"

"Emma," he said. "Your pretty little friend? Beautiful golden eyes? Never heard of her."

Rage tore through Grace's blood. "I know you have her and if you don't tell me where she is, I will find her, and I swear to all the gods, I will kill everyone that steps in my path. Even you, Noah." she retorted, mocking his tone when she said his name.

Noah's smirk faded. "Trust me, Grace, you don't want to go down that road."

Something inside Grace simply snapped. And without even thinking about it, Grace locked her fingers around Noah's throat, and slammed him against the wall, summoning all her magic and strength, forcing him to feel her rage and pain.

"If you've done anything to her, I'll kill you where you stand." For once, Grace saw Noah's confidence and charm waver.

"Grace, please. Let's talk about this, maybe without you crushing my windpipe." Noah was trying to act cool, funny, and well, like him, but Grace could hear his facade faltering. Grace suddenly realized how close they were. Their faces were barely an inch from each other, his tantalizing eyes looked like a cloudy sky. She slowly loosened her grip on his throat, softening. She inhaled his fresh, minty scent that was somehow warm. He reached behind her, reaching for something behind her head. He had picked a light misty pink colored rose. She smiled at it, admiring its beauty and grace. Grace reached out for it, and her hand grazed Noah's. They locked eyes, both not sure of what to do. Then, the sun broke over the mountains, washing them in a golden light. Grace noticed how stunning Noah's eyes look in the lighting, the way they seemed to shift, not blue, not grey, not green, but all of them. In the golden light, Noah and Grace locked eyes, both of their hands on the ravishing flower, and leaned in.

CHAPTER 31

Grace couldn't breathe, she felt dizzy. Her arms were around his neck, the flower still in her hands. One of his hands around her waist, the other touching her hair softly. The kiss was soft, and warm, his lips tasted like vanilla clouds. Grace stirred, pulling away. When they pulled away, they both looked away awkwardly. Grace didn't know what to say. The kiss had made her feel elated, and light, like she could float. It also made her a little sad, for some reason. Maybe because they were both so broken and sad themselves, or maybe because Grace realized she was growing up, that things would never be the same. She guessed it was everything, growing up, losing people, and leaving everything behind. Life would never be the same for Princess Grace Lilian Evans.

Noah looked at her, his eyes sad. "I'll take you to Emma." He assented, looking so defeated and shattered, Grace wanted and wished she could help him. She searched inside herself for some sort of emotion, sadness, maybe sympathy. She wasn't quite sure, instead, she felt ecstatic. She was going to see Emma again! Grace followed Noah out of the garden. Grace seemed to simply glaze over, not paying attention.

"Here." Noah's crisp and cold voice snapped, making Grace startle. Grace noticed how sad Noah looked. She couldn't understand. She figured she would be able to figure out what was going on if she wasn't so distracted. Noah looked worried as well. Grace ignored it and opened the door to Emma's cell. Emma's limp body was wrapped in chains, sprawled across a rickety bed. There was flecks of blood around her wrists from the chains cutting her, and -Grace gasped. Emma's hair had been cut with an axe to shoulder length, the jagged edges of her hair tucked under her. She looked painfully thin, the cloak the Hunters gave her was barely clasped around her neck, it's fabric torn to pieces. Grace wheeled around to face Noah, her hand raised to strike him. She stopped short, seeing his expression. It was a mix of sadness, disdain, and apprehension. Grace realized that he didn't want to see Emma like this as much as she did. Softening, Grace turned back to face Emma. Grace braced herself and entered the cell. Her stomach churned, the smell of blood and damp mold making her light headed and nauseous. Emma started stirring and Grace held her breath.

"Grace, you have to remember, she just died. She won't be the same-" Noah stopped talking because Emma's eyes fluttered open. Emma sat up, her eyes clouded with a misty haze. Her golden eyes were momentarily confused. She opened her mouth to say something, but stopped short. After she seemed to shake off her daze, she opened her mouth again. "Uh, I'm sorry but who are you?" Grace thought this must be some kind of joke. Maybe Emma's words had been directed at Noah. She may have simply forgotten what happened a few hours before her death. Deep down, Grace knew Emma was talking to her. A small part of her tried to fight it, but it was no use. Emma had no memories of anything. Grace's best friend was gone.

CHAPTER 32

Shock was all that registered in Grace. A sickening feeling shot through her stomach. Grace was glad she was empty of tears or she would have curled up right there on the cold cell floor and cried until she died. It broke her. Something inside of her was gone. Shattered. Broken. Dead. Gone forever. She felt empty of any emotion. When Emma had died, Grace felt like she had to stay strong, for Emma, for Olivia, for everyone. Now, she felt like something had broken inside her permanently. Grace stood up abruptly. She walked out of the cell, flicking her hand behind her. Hearing Emma slump to the ground behind her, she kept walking, knowing the spell worked. Grace shoved Noah so hard and with so much force that he fell to the ground. "Gra-" Grace hit him with a blast of light, ensuring that he would be knocked out for at least a day. A darkness so thick and primal, it wiped any thought from her mind. Grace raised her hands, about to release a blast of magic so strong it would kill every single person in this castle. The rage in Grace was replaced by a guilty gut feeling. Her hands fell to her sides. What happened to her? Grace turned around, using her magic to lift up Emma's limp body. She strutted out of the castle, Emma floating behind her. Nobody seemed to see her, so she just kept walking. Grace and Emma reached Grace's horse. Grace conjured ropes and tied Emma to the saddle, so her legs were wrapped around Rose. Her hands were tied to the bag on the side of Rose, securing Emma to the horse. Grace also conjured a blanket, and small pieces of cloth to put under Emma's ropes so she wouldn't get hurt. Grace settled on the saddle, back to back with Emma. Grace spurred Rose, galloping at top speed.

CHAPTER 33

They rode until sunset. When they finally stopped, Grace set up one of the tents Misty had given her. Grace found a source of water, than summoned food for Rose, herself and Emma. She had no idea how she was going to get Emma to eat. Wake her up, tell her to eat, then knock her out again? Or blindfold her and force her to eat? Grace didn't know which would be harder. Grace decided to try the first option. She shook Emma awake, guilt building inside of her already. Emma's eyes opened, and once again, she seemed addled and hazy.

"Eat." Grace said, as gently as she could.

"How do I know this won't kill me?" Emma asked, examining the bread, her voice faint.

Grace felt hurt. "I would never do that to you." Then, her voice quieter, "I lost you once, I wouldn't let that happen again."

Emma bit into the bread and looked around. "Where are we?"

Grace felt sad. "I'll tell you about it later? Eat." Grace responded, her voice a little bit firmer. Emma obviously noticed her tone, because she started eating ravenously, no longer suspicious. Grace watched her wistfully, also eating, though a lot slower. When Emma had finished, she started questioning Grace. "Who are you? Where are we? Who am I? Why should I trust you-" Grace waved her hand impatiently. She sat back, feeling a mix of guilt and satisfaction. Grace waved her hand again, mounting Rose once again, Emma tied behind just like before. She brushed the hair from Emma's face before frowning slightly. Grace slid off of her horse and knelt on the ground. She conjured 5 apples, then summoned all of her willpower, turning the apples to solid gold. Grace made a silent prayer to Aphrodite, then threw the apples into the air, hoping the sacrifice would be enough. She had prayed Olivia and Leo would be okay, since there was enough romance there to hopefully please the goddess of love. Then, Grace prayed that Noah would be okay, that she hadn't killed him with that spell. Grace knew she felt something for Noah, though she didn't like to admit it. She also prayed to Aphrodite to make Emma and herself look presentable. Grace closed her eyes, and when she opened them, she found herself shrouded in a rosy light. Her hair had been curled in perfect ringlets, the diadem perched perfectly on top of her head. Grace was wearing tight black pants, and a red leather blouse that laced up in the front, and wrapped around her shoulders was a black cloak. She pulled out her hunting knife and gasped at her reflection. Black eyeliner, with gold eyeliner stacked on top of it in a perfect wing. Rose red lips, mascara and a dusting of rouge. Grace seemed to glow a shimmery gold. She looked over and saw Emma looked just as good. Grace mounted Rose, and started riding. She knew exactly where she was going, even without a map.

CHAPTER 34

Grace finally made it. The Forest of the Kentaurous. She hopped off of Rose, then unbound Emma and lifted her behind her. Grace heard them before she saw them. The other demigods. Not the Hunters. Just demigods. Grace could sense it, though she didn't ask them. Chiron obviously put them here as guards. The moment Grace heard footsteps, she surrounded Emma in a protective bubble, then floated the bubble far above her head. Grace summoned a steel staff and her hunting knives quickly. They attacked from all sides, an army of them. At the front of the group were obviously the most talented demigods. Grace counted two with swords, one with a bow and arrow, two with spears, and one with 10 throwing knives. Plus that, they all had powers. They weren't like mortals, fighting with swords and spears, they were half god. Fortunately, so was Grace. Grace threw one hunting knife at a swordsman, then the other at a demigod with a spear. She created a force field just as a knife sailed towards her with too much force to be thrown by a human, then dropped to one knee, avoiding the spear thrown at her. The spear sailed over her head and hit the other swordsman. Grace ran towards the demigod with the knives, deflecting the knives with her staff. When she got within striking distance, Grace lashed out with the staff, using her powers to make the hit as hard as she could, and hit the other half blood right on the temple. The demigod crumpled to the ground almost instantly. Grace realized the demigod with the spear was right behind her, spear raised above her head, preparing to strike. Grace raised her staff, to block the spear, only to get shocked with a bolt of electricity. Her arms went numb, and she fell to the ground. Grace's blood boiled, her fingernails drew blood from her palms, and she zeroed in on the half blood in front of her, pinning her eyes on her next victim. Grace began summoning her power, ready to unleash every feeling of anger in her body. Faster than a hairpin trigger, the searing rage in Grace was replaced by a chilly calm. An eerie smile grew on her face, unsettling her opponents more than any power could. Grace unleashed a scream, so shrill and bloodcurdling, her opponents covered their ears and dropped their weapons. Ravens swooped down from every direction, and started ripping out the throats of her enemies, and plucking their eyes out. She then shot a blast of silver across the battlefield, making everyone fall to the ground. They weren't dead, simply in a coma. They would be dead before they woke up, seeing as they were in a thousand year coma. Grace dissolved the staff in her hand and brought Emma down from the sky, feeling glad that Emma did not have to see that. Grace then walked towards the cave entrance, breathing heavily, the adrenaline still pumping through her veins.

CHAPTER 35

"Chiron." Grace called out, surprised by how steely and strong her voice sounded. Here he was. The famous trainer. Chiron was a centaur, with a white body and brown hair, a brown beard, and a brown tail. His dark brown eyes twinkled with wisdom and a deep sadness, as if no one could understand his pain. "Daughter of Artemis. I have been expecting you." Suddenly, Grace felt a sharp, hot stab of pain in her gut. The feeling was so much worse than bringing Emma back to life. It burned so intensely Grace couldn't see. She cried out, doubling over in pain. Chiron draped a necklace over Grace's neck and the pain immediately went away. Grace straightened indignantly. "I see you need training." He said, his voice clear.

"Yes, I do. First, you're going to heal my best friend. I'll make sure of it." Grace snapped.

Printed in the United States
By Bookmasters